Buried in Friendship

A Halflings of Smallburrow
Cozy Fantasy Tale

I0846529

T. M. Mayfield

Copyright Page

Dedication

To my children, especially the one who inspired Eilaen, I love you more than a halfling loves second breakfast. You guys make me strive to be better. Thank you for allowing me to be your mom and giving me the chance to watch you blossom.

A Note from The Author

Buried in Friendship is a cozy story of two neurodiverse friends who set out on a new adventure and find their places, as well as their chosen family, within the town of Smallburrow. Eilaen, who is the POV character in this book, clearly demonstrates autistic traits, as well as traits commonly found in comorbid diagnoses frequently found in those with autism. Kaida, as most will quickly realize, is a character who clearly has ADHD, and Jareth is said to have "no social skills whatsoever", and struggles with social cues and societal norms, which is something we will see more of in his book, *Rooted in Magic*.

As an author with AudHD, as well as a mother to children with a variety of combinations involving ADHD, Autism, and dyslexia, it is important to me that my children, as well as others, grow up with characters in a fantasy setting that they can relate to. While more YA and adult fantasy is incorporating these themes, as well as mental heath themes, it's not really something we've found in middle grade and lower YA fantasy. And thus, Smallburrow was born, as were these flawed, unreliable-in-their-narrations characters, all of whom have their own struggles (both internal and external) with their neurodiversities.

No two neurodiverse individuals are the same, which is worth noting to readers as they embark upon their Smallburrow journey. Please note that this is also reflected in our characters. Thank you so much for reading this story. I hope you enjoy your visit to our cozy little slice of fantasy heaven.

Table of Contents

A Most Peculiar Morning

Something is going to change today. Go back to bed, don't get up. Change is coming and you can't handle that.

Today feels weird. I can't tell if it's the air or if it's me as a halfling. But there is something about today that isn't the same as it always is. Every morning when I wake, I follow the same routine. I get up, make my bed, and then get dressed. A glance at the calendar on my wall tells me that there are officially two months left until my birthday, which guarantees that Kaida, my closest friend, hasn't done anything that could be constituted as a surprise. The slow and easy pace I've grown to expect is still here, but something just isn't...

Shaking my head to clear my thoughts, I stomp down the stairs, making a quick stop in the pantry once I reach the bottom. After I collect my breakfast items, I exit the closet-sized room and turn left into my kitchen. Carefully, I set the items in my hand onto the table and pour fresh water into the iron kettle I fill every morning for my cup of tea before slathering two slices of bread with butter and frying them in the pan I use for breakfast.

Once the buttered sides are a nice, golden brown, I sit at the table with the toast and a new jar of homemade apple jam. It's a routine I have worked very hard to solidify over the years and one I cannot have interrupted. It's the only thing I know I can rely on being consistent without fail. Just as I pick up the knife to spread the jam across the first slice of toast, a noise startles me. Footsteps scrape across the dirt pathway as someone shuffles closer to my front door.

I jump from my seat, my feet hitting the floor harder than I'd like. When I make it to the window, my eyes widen from the shock of seeing an elderly man outside. Eyebrows scrunched, I step across the room to the door as I mutter to myself. "Whoever could that be?"

Interactions this early in the day interrupt my train of thought and make me extremely uncomfortable. As I wait for the mysterious caller to approach my door, my stomach knots as my pulse races in anticipation. Even Kaida allows me an hour or so to wake and eat breakfast before attempting to interact with me.

I open the door slowly, hoping it'll allow me the extra time to get a closer look at the stranger. He's short, but not too short. His cropped hair is white as snow, and there are wrinkles around his brown eyes that make me think he's someone who smiles a lot. This loosens the tension in my chest enough to breathe. I always like interacting with people who smile a lot, and I frequently find joy in their smiles.

My eyes wander to the bright yellow tunic he wears, which he has paired with dark brown trousers. Oddly enough, I notice that his feet are completely bare, yet they show no sign of being dirty. I wonder how far he traveled from… well, wherever it was that he had come from.

Still confused, I plaster a smile onto my face as I address him. "Hello. May I help you?" she asked.

"Yes, Miss. I am looking for a Halfling by the name of, uh, Enid? Last name Mapleground. I have a letter for delivery," he replies, his words rough and gravely. For a moment, I almost wonder if I should invite him in for a cup of tea to soothe it, though I quickly decide against it.

"Erm, m-my name is Eilaen. Long "e" in front of "lane". You know, like a road? That's me. I am Eilaen Mapleground," I stammer, thrusting my hand towards him awkwardly.

It's only when he hands me the letter that I notice the sadness in his eyes. Another look at him has me tilting my head as I realize the smile on his face may not be one of happiness. Facial expressions have always been confusing to me, so I'm not surprised I didn't notice at first that his face is what I've learned to associate with looks of pity.

No longer able to pretend to maintain eye contact, I cast my eyes down to the wrinkled envelope between my fingers. My hands shake when I notice the sender's name is that of my estranged grandfather. Again, my stomach clenches from all of the unknown variables involved in this peculiar meeting.

When I finally tear my eyes away from my grandfather's name, I realize the man has disappeared. I turn my head to the left, then to the right, as I try to see where he went, but I can see no sign of him. It's as if he has completely vanished into thin air, not even leaving footprints in the dirt beneath my feet. If it wasn't for the mysterious letter in my hand, I know I would be convincing myself that this exchange had been nothing more than a figment of my imagination. With my empty hand, I massage my wrinkled forehead before turning around and closing the door after stepping into my house.

As I shuffle my way to the kitchen once more, I slide my finger under the sealed envelope, but I cannot finish opening it. I hear the scream of my iron kettle whistling, and I startle forward, almost tripping over my large feet as I rush to the stove top to put out the first apparatus that it rests on.

The scene I return to reminds me that I was interrupted during my breakfast routine. After I take a deep breath to recenter myself, I pour the hot water over the tea leaf concoction in my cup. I take a second deep breath as the heavenly scent of butterscotch fills the air, the steam swirling above the teacup delicately. Unable to wait any longer, I rip the envelope open. Surprisingly, I find that I am eager to read the contents of it, even though I'm not sure what to expect. Jellied toast in one hand and the letter in the other, I scan the first paragraph. It's definitely my grandfather's handwriting.

I'm not sure why I would have expected any differently, considering it's his name and seal on the envelope, but I had. I still recognize his handwriting; I'd know it anywhere, the crisp lettering imprinted into my mind from the plethora of discarded envelopes and letters. Letters that had been addressed to my father, arriving week after week. I was certain my father would eventually read one of them. Instead, I remember being puzzled each time he threw them into the fireplace, all being discarded without being opened.

By the time I'm stuffing the last bite of toast into my mouth, I'm halfway through my third read through of Grandfather Mapleground's letter.

No matter how hard I try, I cannot process the words in front of me. Due to the differing opinions regarding my father's chosen profession, my father and grandfather had a brutal falling out almost twenty years ago, when I was nothing more than a toddling halfling. To my knowledge, my grandfather had never reached out to me.

And yet... Now that he's dead, he wants to pass down the family farm? To *me*? The world spins before my eyes, my head getting increasingly heavy with each pass. Panic bubbles inside me, and it's like there's a large animal that has taken residence on my chest.

I need to get out of the house. I need to get into town, find Kaida, and get her thoughts. There isn't anyone else I'd trust more to give me advice than my best friend and sole confidant. *If anyone knows what to do, it'll be her.*

As I finish my cup of tea, I run through the questions I need to ask her. There's so much that can change, and I honestly don't know how much of that I can handle. My heart races harder, my blood pulsing in my skull. My chest aches from how hard I'm breathing. I don't even realize I've already made it to the front door until my hand is on the handle. Ripping the door open, I step outside, almost forgetting to lock the door behind me. I catch it before it latches closed, twisting the little bronze knob on the inside with one hand while patting my pocket to feel for my key with the other. Though I force myself to slow down, the sense of urgency is still present within each step, thought, and motion I proceed with as I make my way down the dust-covered road towards Galbassi.

I knew things were going to change when I woke up to the air feeling wrong today, and now I can't stop thinking about what that'll mean for me.

A Pastry for Your Thoughts

Kaida's Bakery is busier than normal this morning, the noise washing over me when I step inside. The calming scent of pastries and freshly baked bread mingle as I take a deep breath, leaving me with more peace than I've had since opening my eyes this morning. My eyes dart around the room as I take stock of how long I'll have to wait in line. From what I can see, there are two Halflings ahead of me in line, one waiting to be served, and one more that stepped inside after I did.

Kaida, a complete wiz of a baker, is a half-elf, half-halfling. She inherited her height from her halfling mother and her magic from her elf father. Her hair is the same shade of green as the leaves in the springtime, stopping at the halfway point between her chin and her shoulders. With an angled face that slightly rounds out at her chin and eyes the color of sparkling sapphires, her ears are the most elvish part of her appearance and poke out from behind her hair, though it's just enough so that you can see their pointed tips. Though she's swift and agile thanks to her elvish lineage, she's also stocky and round like her halfling mother. Her favorite joke to make is that being a full-time baker doesn't help her reach her elvish potential of being lean and lithe, though I know she is more than comfortable in her own skin. If I had to describe her to someone, I would tell them that Kaida is the kindest, bubbliest, most energetic being in the village of Galbassi.

I've always said that Kaida's love language is feeding

people, and she's well-known by all who know her for ensuring that her friends never do without the baked goods that she knows we love so dearly. The Galbassi council has even dubbed her the best baker the town has ever had the privilege of having; this gives her the advantage of having a storefront, even though most bakers in town sell their goods from their kitchen windows. Some townsfolk murmur that it's her baking magic that allows her to never create a badly baked good. Others, however, say that it's nothing short of her attention to detail and her inability to focus on anything other than whatever it is that she is baking. Honestly, I don't care what it is or isn't that allows her to bake whatever she sets her mind to. I'm just happy that I get the chance to enjoy the fruits of her labor as her unofficial taste tester.

When it comes to the townsfolk, everyone knows where they stand with Kaida, especially since she's never afraid to be outspoken when necessary. She's been my shoulder to cry on for as long as I can remember, never failing to hold her hand through the good times and the bad. Out of all of the possible changes that the farm could cause, the worst is that I will have to leave Kaida behind in Galbassi. My heart aches as the thought, and for the first time, I wonder if you can actually die from a broken heart. But as much as that hurts, I know there's no way I will ever be able to ask her to leave the bakery she puts her heart and soul into every day.

I stand in line, taking deep breath after deep breath, allowing the buttery goodness of whatever bread Kaida has in the oven to fill me. By the time I make it to the counter, I have to wipe my chin to make sure I haven't been drooling without realizing it. Sounds come from the kitchen, the distinct clang of metal hitting concrete echoing across the store, a signal that Kaida's in there whipping up something new. The sounds of her baking are accompanied by the frustrated growls and loud complaints of dropping an egg into the floor and a bowl onto her foot. Somehow, I manage to resist the laughter bubbling inside me, knowing that she isn't going to be very pleasant if I'm cackling when she walks out here and hears what I found funny enough to laugh at.

After a few moments, the familiar noises that have been coming from within the kitchen stop. I watch as her form appears in the doorway. Effortlessly, she glides through the double doors separating the kitchen and its heat from the customers in the dining area, a platter of hot, gooey brownies that she carries perfectly balanced in each hand. When she sees me standing at the counter, her eyes light up in recognition and a smile spreads across her face. As soon as the customer behind me pays and walks outside, she unties her apron, tosses it to the side, and bounces toward me.

She pivots to the left and grabs two lemon raspberry tarts, which she knows are my favorite summer pastry of hers. Before she tries to convince me not to pay for them, I plan out my counter argument for when she tries to offer them for free.

"Don't even think about it, Kaida. Every time I come in here, I have to remind you that you have to buy the ingredients to make the tarts but you also need to pay yourself for the work you put into them." When she opens her mouth, I continue speaking. "No. You aren't winning this one today, Kai. I'm paying. You wouldn't allow me last week so you can't stop me today."

I fold my arms across my chest defiantly and raise my eyebrow, practically begging her to attempt to change my mind. She and I both know, however, that I won't be budging on this.

"You are worth the expense, you know," I tell her, with a smile. "I'd rather support you than anyone else. We both know that."

"Fine," she says, grumbling. Triumphantly, I take the treats from her hands and we walk over to an empty table, wasting no time before plopping into our seats.

"What's up, Buttercup?" Kaida asks, looking at me suspiciously. "What's bothering you, Ellie?"

"There has been a recent development and it will cause a big change," I reply slowly. "I need some help, Kai." I take a large bite, not looking up from my tart. I pick at the crumbs on my napkin, the flakey crust melting in my mouth.

"Okay, so talk to me. What's going on?" She cocks her head to the side, her perfectly manicured green brows furrowing.

Chewing on my lip, I hesitate for a moment before slipping

the letter out of my pocket, handing it to her as I silently wait for her to read it. Anxiously, I pick at my cuticles as I wait to hear Kaida's thoughts. Her eyes dart back and forth across the page as she reads the letter twice, each time in its entirety, before laying the parchment down on the table. Looking up at me, she takes a deep breath in preparation to give me her thoughts.

"Well Ellie, it appears as if we have an adventure beginning." Her wide smile beams at me.

"What do you mean we have an adventure beginning?" I ask, my eyebrow raising as I stare at her, bewildered.

Surely she doesn't mean...

"What does it sound like, Eilaen? I mean, do you honestly think that I would allow you to make such a large change all alone? Don't be so ridiculous! I'll have to make other arrangements for the bakery, of course, but that won't be too hard. I definitely think it's doable. This is the adventure of a lifetime, Ellie. If I'm being completely honest, I think we would be crazy to not consider it." Kaida's smile softens as her hands wrap around mine and she squeezes gently.

"Don't you want to see it first? I mean, before making your decision to move? We have no idea what we're even walking into with this farm. I haven't been there since I was a toddling tot, and my memories of the farm are clouded by time. I don't even know how long it's been since anyone has inhabited it," I ask, still confused by her willingness to drop everything and leave.

To be honest, I thought that Kaida would suggest we take a day trip so we could look at the farm, and then I would try to talk her out of it on our way back to Galbassi. I should have known better because Kaida lives by the seat of her trousers, never thinking twice about the jump before taking the leap.

The whole idea of moving and starting over somewhere is more than terrifying. It will change everything I know, and the familiar tightening of panic spreads through my chest. This is becoming too much, too quickly. I wish more than anything that I could turn back time to when I woke this morning with the knowledge I currently possess. If I could change anything, I would simply stay in bed all day, perhaps feigning an illness to avoid meeting the stranger who delivered the letter.

My breaths come faster with each passing heartbeat, and it doesn't take long for me to get overwhelmed. I'm obviously not going to take this transition well, considering nothing has happened and I'm already about to fall apart.

With my thoughts racing, I sit in front of Kaida and listen as she chatters about how grand it could be if we were to pick up our entire lives to move to a town neither of us have lived in. Galbassi is the only home we know, and I'm not sure if I will ever be okay with that changing. The thunder of Kaida's voice echoing through me pulls me back to the conversation.

"Just think about it, Ellie. After all, weren't we recently talking about how great a new start would be? A new start, one that could bring us a new purpose. Call me crazy, but I think this could really be our chance?" Kaida's question has so much hope spoken into it as she tries to encourage me to think about the opportunity we've been presented.

"I know, Kai. I know. The thing is... I can't just... It- it's just that this isn't some small, insignificant thing. It's something huge. It's a major change. One that would be completely life altering. This is big and new and... scary," I whisper. I can hear the wobble in my voice as tears burn in my eyes. Overwhelmed, I draw in a shaky breath as I try to keep from crying.

"I know it is, Eilaen." Kaida's hand stretches across the table and grasps mine comfortingly. "I promise. I do. However, it's also important to remember that just because it is scary and new and big doesn't mean that it's going to be bad," Kaida's tone is soothing as she does her best to reassure me that this isn't a worse case scenario situation.

Still, I reluctantly nod as I promise to think about it, but only if she agrees to go with me the next day so we can look at the farm and assess. As impulsive as she may be, Kaida's thought process in this makes sense to me, even if I don't want it to. When a large group walks through the door, we both stand, hugging before Kaida picks our napkins up off of the table.

Thanks to Kaida, I'm breathing easier than I have since waking, and I'm definitely less anxious now that we've spoken. I relax, noting how the tension has left my shoulders as I approach the glass counter and purchase a dozen lemon raspberry tarts.

The air outside is even crisp, I notice, as I walk through the bakery door and outside again.

As I walk down the dusty stretch of road home, my mind is plagued with the mental listing of the pros and cons that could potentially come should we proceed to move to Smallburrow. The longer the list grows, the more my stomach knots up in apprehension.

I hope Grandpa knew what he was doing when he decided I'm the best person to take over the farm, even though I have no idea what goes into being a farmer or taking care of livestock and plants. How would I even begin to start learning what will need to be done? Will there be any neighbors around that could help?

The harsh reality of it all slams into me almost as soon as my feet hit my lawn. *Maybe this isn't going to be such a good idea in the long run,* my mind whispers to me, reminding me of every plant death I've caused in the last two years. By those standards, I'm the last halfling who needs to be in charge of plants. Especially when one takes into consideration that I can't even keep the easiest to care for hovel-plant alive, for halfling's sake! Is it truly going to be possible for me to keep an entire garden's worth of plants alive and thriving?

With a sigh, I slip the small brass key into the keyhole of the same color, closing the door quietly behind me before making a beeline to my sofa. After picking my current read up from the table beside me, I drag my favorite blanket over my legs, I snuggle against the cushions in hopes that it will allow my racing mind to relax, even if only while I escape into the fictional world in my hands.

Two Halflings and a Horse Stroll onto a Farm

When I wake, Kaida's pounding on my door. Groggily, I make the short trip down the hallway and answer, only to see she's already hooked my horse, Mable, up to the wagon. On the bench seat is something flakey and fruity, the steam drifting off of it indicating the love Kaida put into treating me this morning. It doesn't take us long before we're ready to leave towards Smallburrow, and most importantly, the farm.

The anxious energy we harbor has us buzzing as we travel, though I know hers is more excited while mine is nerves. Truthfully, I'm not sure if I'll be able to emotionally or mentally handle the changes should we like what we see. As we get closer, we discuss our plans. Kaida tells me every minute detail in her pursuit of starting a cottage bakery, down to hiring a head baker for her bakery in Galbassi.

"If I can hire someone to work the counter and bus tables, I should only need one baker. It'll cut into my profits, but it could also allow me to save up what I need so that I can open a second shop in Smallburrow. Between selling breads and pastries, as well as whatever farm fresh goodies you actually get to survive to be harvested, we should also be able to make enough to keep the farm running."

"You're probably not wrong, Kai," I reply, mulling it over.

I love that she has such big dreams, but I genuinely have yet to figure out what I would want to gain from this new adventure. But since Kaida seems set on following this through, I suppose I'll have to figure it out sooner rather than later. It's clear from how excitedly she talks that she's made up her mind that this is the only way forward, and when Kaida sets her course, only a major catastrophe can alter the way. And all of this without knowing what state the land or cottage are in!

As she continues to chatter away, I sigh, wishing I had the courage to be more like her. Though I've always wished to be, I'm nothing like Kaida who can do anything she wants to do on a whim. Instead, I need to have everything planned out, even down to the smallest potential change. Everything in my life has a place and time. When plans are made, they have to be carried out exactly as said. This means that every obstacle has to be accounted for or I tend to work myself into an emotional frenzy. I heave another sigh when I notice I have, yet again, gotten lost in thought.

It doesn't matter how badly I want to be spontaneous, I tell myself. It's simply not within my ability. One of these days, maybe I'll be able to accept the way I am and save myself the mental anguish that comes with wishing to be someone else.

When we arrive at the farm, our tentative plans have been solidified. So long as the farm needs no repairs, we should be able to have all of our belongings completely moved in by the end of the month. Which only gives me two weeks to both plan and process. That should be enough time to convince myself that moving is going to be as great of an idea as Kaida is convinced it will be, right? As we pull into the large farm, I whisper a hope that I will be just as in love with this grand adventure as Kaida is. Either that, or I better get really good at pretending.

As I pull the reigns connecting Mabel to the wagon and we slow to a stop, I look out at the sight before us. Even Kaida is struck silent. The landscape is gorgeous and nothing like I can recall having ever seen before. To the left are rows upon rows of vegetables, most just barely poking out of the freshly packed dirt. The rich scent of damp soil permeates the air around us. Just a small handful of steps behind the vegetable garden are dozens of bushes and trees, appearing to contain many different varieties of fruit.

To the right of the property is a large barn and I quickly see that there's a chicken coop beside it. The sounds and smells of hay, pigs, cows, and chickens drift across the yard, filling the air and assaulting my olfactory system. Tightly situated between the barn and coop is what appears to be a stable that houses a donkey. From where I sit, I suspect it should also have enough room for Mable. A wooden shed that has been well stocked with split logs is attached to the right side of the coop and I barely notice a trough sitting just to the left of the barn.

Directly in front of us is a well worn path extending just beyond the gate and at the end of the pathway is the farmhouse. Looking at it, I'm not sure what I was expecting, but it definitely wasn't the magnificent house in front of me. Unlike my little hole in the ground, this house looks as if it should belong in a storybook rather than on this plot of land. On the outside, large slabs of stone have been arranged in a pattern that stretches from the exterior's top down to bottom. The brown slated roof has a stone chimney that looks as if it has been placed over what seems to be either the den or kitchen, though it's hard to be sure without being inside.

Dark, leafy green ivy climbs up the exterior, intricately winding upwards, circling around the posts on both sides of the doorway, both of which support the awning that covers the steps on our side of the front door. Every one of the windows are round and large, and the largest of them overlooks the flower garden. On the left side of the walkway is a large, stone well that seems to have been crafted from the same stone slabs as the house, making it almost identical in appearance. There are even several of the same ivy vines twisting around the steepled top of it.

Behind the well and alongside the house are flower beds that are currently overflowing with flowers of all shapes, colors, and sizes. Hovering effortlessly over the flowers are an array of colorful butterflies, the group mingling beautifully with bumblebees and dragonflies. Though the scents of the flowers mix together, I somehow manage to detect the slightest hints of roses and hydrangeas. Most of the other flowers, I quickly notice, are some that I've never seen and I decide to get a book on floral gardens so that I can identify them more efficiently.

As I climb out of the wagon, I see that on the left exterior of the house is a large herb garden full of basil, rosemary, cilantro, and thyme. The subtlest hint of garlic is also faintly present, growing stronger as I get closer to it, making me wonder if there is some wild garlic nearby. Before I get much further, squeals of delight reach my ears.

"Eilaen! There is a gigantic round window that looks like it's in the kitchen window. And it looks like it's overlooking the herb garden," she shouts to me, jumping up and down.

Before we enter the house, I release Mable from the wagon and walk her to the fence where I can tie her to a post. I'm more than a little relieved when I see that there is still a bucket inside of the well and I quickly fill it with water and place it in front of her before turning toward the house.

Cautiously, Kaida and I walk up to the front door. "Are you ready?" She asks me.

Wordlessly, I nod and dig around in my pocket. After pulling out the keyring consisting of three different keys that somehow magically appeared at my table last night, I take a moment to compose myself. I inhale a deep breath and slowly exhale it before finally sliding the house key into the keyhole. With trembling hands, I slowly twist the key, turning the knob after hearing the click from the lock mechanisms sliding into place. Slowly, the door opens and the hinges screech loudly as it swings wider.

Kaida and I exchange a look and after she gives me an encouraging smile, I take the first step inside, making a conscious decision to stop once I'm inside the doorway. Whispy images of forgotten memories only fill my mind as I push myself further inside, and I take care to swipe my feet against the mat taking up space in the walkway. Kaida follows my lead and, together, we turn to the left and walk into the den.

There are three large chairs with a matching sofa that have been arranged in front of the fireplace for optimal seating, all looking worn in perfectly, as well as a bookshelf that has been placed symmetrically on either side of the mantle. In front of the hearth lays a worn brown and green rug, and I can almost imagine someone spending many hours of their life pacing back and forth along its length. The air in the room is comforting instead of musty, nostalgia filling each breath I take in. With my eyes closed, I can picture sitting in front of a crackling fire on a snowy winter night, cups of hot cocoa in one hand and a good book in the other. The scents of the burning wood and warm, rich chocolate are so strong that I can almost believe they'll be there when my eyes open again.

On the other side of the den is a short, wide hallway with two doors on the sides and trenches into the kitchen. The door on the right flings open when Kaida reaches it, and we lean in to find it's a sizable walk-in closet that has a mountain of throw blankets and plush decorative pillows that match every season possible. As Kaida's hands rhythmically slap together enthusiastically over the new-to-her decorative pieces, I turn to the second door and slowly open it.

Inside, I find a study with a large, dark mahogany desk and its equally large, dark mahogany chair. Stacks of parchment, ink pots, and several quills sit on the top, almost as if they are still waiting on a pair of hands to sit at the desk and resume their writing projects. The smallish room still carries the faintest scents of old parchment, pipe tobacco, and leather. I take a moment to inhale deeply, savoring the lingering smells as they mix together in their journey through my olfactory system.

Lining the far wall is a line of bookshelves, each holding a massive collection of books on farming, flower gardens, animal husbandry, and household maintenance. There are far too many titles for me to get a complete grasp of the library I'm standing in front of, and I mentally note my want to come back through and better look through the books. Still, as I move away from them, I cannot help but consider all the ways I can utilize the organized space to read or write, a warm and fuzzy feeling spreading through my entire body.

None of what I have seen has anything less than extraordinary, the idea of us living here becoming a real possibility with each step further. "Kaida, this house is incredible. I never knew that there would be so much here for us." My eyes find her, meeting them as she pokes her head out of the closet.

Excitement gets the best of me as I continue. "We wouldn't even have to pack the heavy furniture!"

Kaida's infectious laughter echoes through the hallway, her head bobbing in agreement. As I predicted on our trip, she and I are of the same mind when it comes to condensing and combining our things together – it's nothing either of us is interested in doing. If we stay—and this is me reminding myself it is still an if at this point—not having this daunting task in front of us is another check in the quickly growing list of pros.

Together, we backtrack to the den before making our way across the entryway, turning into the dining room. A large table sits directly in the center of the room, appearing to have been made from the same dark mahogany wood that the desk in the study was crafted from. Surrounding it are enough chairs to seat a dozen people. I approach it, dragging my fingers through the swirls and dips carved into it in full appreciation of the intricate details. The craftsmanship that created this work of art is unlike anything I can recall seeing. Whoever the craftsman was had obviously taken great lengths to create such a beautiful set, doing so in a way that has given it the ability to last a lifetime.

The dining room archway ahead of us opens directly into the kitchen, which is the next stop on our tour. With no more than a step into the room, I stop as I take in the sight before me. The kitchen was the largest I have seen, and a glance towards my best friend tells me that she's equally as impressed. When her eyes meet mine, I take note of how astounded she is.

Three of the four walls are lined with counters and pristine butcher blocks as the countertops. The surfaces are worn, yet they've obviously been well taken care of. To the left side of the kitchen is an older wood stove. Across the room is the large, rounded window we had seen outside that overlooks the herb garden. On our side of the window is the kitchen sink, making it possible so that one can look upon the spoils of their labor as they wash dishes if they wish.

In the center of the room is a large island, the top of which perfectly matches the counters. A walk around it shows that it's still well stocked with all the equipment necessary to bake anything the mind could concoct. In the cabinet on the side are shelves of bowls, whisks, rolling pins, and cookie cutters properly organized. Somewhere in the distance, I can hear the nonexistent echoes of a memory of the sounds of my grandmother baking, as well as smell the distant scent of bread as it bakes.

Dramatically, Kaida clutches her chest with a gasp. "I have *died*, Ellie. I have died and found myself in a heaven that was created solely for bakers. As my best friend, you are required to bury me with my whisks and pans. And don't forget my apron. I'm going to need it!"

I practically have to drag Kaida's salivating body out so we can check out the upstairs rooms. With me in front, we climb the steps, stopping next to one another on the landing that leads to the hallway. On each side of the hallway, there are two doors. Both doors on the right and the second to the left all lead to bedrooms, the three of them mostly bare and contain nothing more than a single bed, a nightstand, and dresser in each.

Like the table, desk, and chairs downstairs, the frames and dressers have been handcrafted, each piece of furniture created beautifully. With a sigh, I drop onto one of the mattresses and find that they're surprisingly comfortable, though they are all on the thinner side. Each of the three rooms are every detail, down to the very layout of each down to the wall color and light fixtures.

The bathing room is behind the remaining door, positioned at the end of the hall. Coincidentally, it's next to the room Kaida has chosen to be hers, though I'm not sure why. Inside is a wooden tub. Connected to the tub is a hose that has been threaded through the wall which allows the water to drain out automatically, a toilet, a sink with a water pump, and a miniature wooden stove with a matching kettle to warm the water with. I'm not sure how they managed this, but my grandparents were ahead of their years with the way they built it.

Even if I was leaning towards not moving into this house, there's no way Kaida is going to let me pass on the opportunity and the realization slams into me as I stand in the entryway once more. This chance is too perfect for us to pass up, but even with this knowledge, it doesn't take long for the all-too familiar tightness to build in my chest as it threatens to spread through me.

As we stumble through the front door and out into the front yard, we officially make the decision that moving to the farm will be every bit worth the changes it will bring. After taking a few breaths to steady myself, the constriction in my chest loosens and the butterflies in my chest settle, the excitement now growing by the minute. Before I have the chance to verbalize my thoughts, I see a victorious grin on Kaida's face, and I know she can see the change of heart I've felt. Thankfully, I also know she'll be at my side through the good and the bad that this will bring me.

A New Beginning

It takes the entire two weeks we had planned, but we somehow manage to get everything taken care of. As Kaida spends most of her time interviewing new bakers, I take stock of everything I want to take with me, logging it meticulously by category. It's the little things like planning that calm me when my stomach clenches and my chest weighs with panic. I keep myself so busy preparing for our new lives on the farm, the days pass by quickly, and with little time to overthink the changes coming so quickly.

Until the night before we are set to leave, that is. Somehow, I forgot to factor in saving something for me to do on my final night in my special hole in the ground, the place I have lived for the last five years. Tears in my eyes, I walk around the one-story home one final time, allowing the nostalgia to flow through me as stray tears drip down my face.

Nothing of value remains in any room, other than the bedroll I'll be sleeping on tonight. Everything else has been loaded onto the wagon, filling every nook and cranny that Kaida's left unfilled. Each step I take, every breath I inhale, and all of the involuntary movements I fail to recognize every day echo far too loudly. Slowly, I unroll the bedroll and climb into it, and lie down as the bittersweet taste of my last night of normalcy clings to me, knowing that I'll be sleeping in my room one last time.

A deep sigh escapes me as the realization settles in, and I instantly know sleep will be hard to come by tonight. In the depths of the silent night, so many memories of my life in Galbassi flood through my mind. The first memory I cannot move past plays, and I see myself as I was when I moved in five years ago, only months after my parents died in a fire that burned through the business district.

Though I try to shut it down as quickly as possible, it doesn't stop my mind as it reels wildly out of control. I try not to think of my parents, knowing that the grief will weigh heavily and that the feelings rarely fit back into the inner box I keep them neatly locked inside. More tears prickle my eyes and I wish that, more than anything, they were still here for encouragement and support. A large tear slides down the side of my face, and I wipe it away, sniffling as I close my eyes and hope that sleep will come faster than I fear it will.

It must have finally come for me, because one moment I'm counting my one hundredth sheep and the next I'm being startled awake with the sound of a loud voice, warm sunshine pouring through the window, and the scent of a warm, fresh raspberry lemon tart drifting down the hallway. Kaida's here.

With a loud yawn, I sit up and rub the bleary sleep from my eyes, looking outside the bedroom window for the last time. The sky brightens before me as the sun stretches over the tops of the trees, waking the birds who are now chirping their songs in the distance. Unfortunately for me, the morning's beauty and cheer aren't quite as warm and bright within me. Instead, I'm just as sad as I was when I was falling asleep last night, the bitterness of what I'm trading just as strong as I imagined it would be when I was lying awake and staring at the moon. With a groan, I stretch as I stand and roll my bedding back into the log-like shape it started as.

Before I make it from my room, Kaida's voice breaks through the silence, the sing-song tone ringing on the end of every other word. "Wake up, sleepy head! It's time to rise and shine so that we can get this show on the road!" She glides to a stop in front of me. "I don't want to have to live out of bags. We need to have time to put away our things because I am dying to make some fresh bread to go with some of your infamous potato soup."

She's vibrating with pure excitement, barely able to keep herself from bounding on the balls of her feet. "You sound like a yappy bird chirping in the sunshine, Kai. So peppy. So loud. So unnecessarily wide awake." My mouth stretches into a yawn as I reposition my bedroll and walk outside to where my best friend stands in wait by the wagon.

She takes my bedding with one hand as the other extends towards me with her peace offering–a stack of raspberry lemon tarts–smiling at me with false sincerity. "And you, my dear Ellie, sound exactly as I would expect a cranky bat to when they are ready to sleep the day away." With a grunt, she tosses the bedding into the wagon and then bounces up to the bench a moment later.

Before I get in next to her, I look the wagon over from back to front, not failing to notice that Kaida has not only already grabbed Mable, but has also hitched her to the wagon. And she managed to do it before she even walked into the house this morning to wake me.

How I found someone so wonderful to be my best friend and platonic soulmate, I will never know, and will always be thankful for.

Between bites, I thank her for all of her work, taking care to brush the crumbs from my hands as I put the final bite into my mouth. Climbing up into the seat beside Kaida, I take the reins. Slowly, I look around and clear my throat.

"Onto our adventure?" I ask, trying to keep the dread from my voice, choosing to look at Kaida's smiling face to remind me why I'm doing this. Her grin widens as she nods vigorously in agreement. With a squeal of excitement from Kaida, we officially set off to our new home, leaving Galbassi in the dust behind us.

One stop and half a day later, we finally arrive at the farmhouse in Smallburrow. With a nimbleness that one would only consider to be of the elves, Kaida leaps from her seat. Behind her, I slowly climbed down, sparks of pain running from my hips to my knees. It's going to take ages for me to work the stiffness out of my body after a long trip.

Side by side, we stand in front of the gate, our hands planted firmly on our hips as we take in the sight before us. This is now our home, I tell myself. The most surprising part of it all is how much like home it already feels, leaving me wondering whether that's from the legacy of my grandparents or if it's my body's way of telling me that everything is going to be okay. I see my reflection in Kaida's large eyes, surprised to see that my eyes match hers in wonderment, but I don't ruin the moment by asking if she feels the butterflies in her stomach the same way that I do.

Not wanting to give myself time to overthink anything, I quickly set off to unhitch Mabel and lead her down the side of the house and towards the barn, where the water trough sits near the stable. Kaida decides to take on the task of unpacking our things from the wagon, carrying items into the house. After making sure Mable has what she needs, I half-walk, half-jog back to the front of the house so that I can assist. Maybe we'll be able to get everything into the house before the sun begins to set.

The thought crosses my mind again and again of how grateful I am that the farmhouse was given to me fully furnished, enabling them to travel lighter without any large pieces of furniture. After the wagon has been completely emptied, we stand in the den once more.

"So, where do we start?" Kaida asks, weariness coating her words as her mouth opens in a yawn.

Looking around at the overwhelming mess causes my insides to quiver and makes my skin prickle as if ants were crawling all over me. It's almost so uncomfortable that I barely register the ferocity with which my stomach grumbles until Kaida's giggles burst from behind her hand. My hands fly to my abdomen as another rumble rips through me, this time bringing a small bout of nausea with it.

Due to the trip, we haven't eaten nearly as much today as we typically do and it's finally hitting me. "We need to move whatever groceries we have into the kitchen so that I can see what we have and what I may need to get from out in the garden," I tell Kaida as I grab the first basket of vegetables.

Once everything is where it should be in the kitchen, I leave the kitchen so Kaida can get into the zone and get herself together so she can get the dough for the bread going, as well as decide on what she wants to make for the two of us for dessert.

I linger just long enough to watch the beginning of the

process; it's one that never fails to leave any witness amazed. After a moment, I wander outside with a basket I found hanging on the wall by the door. My feet effortlessly find their way to the garden and I'm once again amazed by the sheer beauty in front of me.

How has it only been two weeks since we were last here? Since then, the plants have somehow grown exponentially, almost as if aided by magic. I've heard of such magic, though I've never been able to see it before. In Galbassi, such magic is only seen in rare cases, and usually only if one happens to be of a family or race explicitly known for their magical lineage. Even then, I can only think of a small handful of Galbassians with magic and Kaida is probably the only one I know personally who uses her magic so openly.

I allow myself to drift through the rows of vegetables, unable to stop my fingers from grazing everything on both sides, the basket hanging in the crook of my elbow as I do. The vast array of produce growing in front of me is unlike any selection I have seen in one place. It's genuinely astounding.

Carrots, tomatoes, radishes, and cabbage alternated the rows in the two largest plots, while lettuce, beans, beets, and snap peas made up another plot. If I take three steps forward, I come to two plots that each contain four rows of corn stalks with two mounds of potatoes on the other side, in an even smaller plot. Basket in hand, I reach down to harvest something–anything– but hesitate. I don't know how to tell if they're all ripe for harvest, so I take a deep breath and hope for the best before grabbing five carrots, three large heirloom tomatoes, two handfuls each of beans and peas, three ears of corn, and six medium potatoes.

Before going inside, I walk to the herb garden and grab small handfuls of both basil and rosemary for taste. This soup is going to be incredible, I can feel it!

With glee, I practically skip into the house, taking care to wipe my feet on the doormat so I don't track dirt inside. The comforting scent of fresh bread greets me the moment the door opens, the scent becoming increasingly more enticing with each step I take to the kitchen. If my mouth waters any more, I'll be cleaning up a puddle from the floor.

"Hey! I left a pot on the stove so you can make the potatoes," she says over her shoulder.

After thanking her, I head to the sink and dump the basket of vegetables into it so I can wash the dirt off of them before prepping them. As I finish peeling the last potato, a snap echoes across the kitchen from Kaida's fingers, and two clouds of salt and ground pepper float above our heads into the pot, allowing me to brown the small amount of pork sausage I brought with us.

"Kaida, that was incredible. How did I not know you could do party tricks like that? We've been as close as sisters almost our entire lives and yet I see you're hiding new tricks from me," I tease, a fake scowl on my face—barely

With as much sass as possible, Kaida replies, "That's not all I have recently learned to do. Watch this!"

Carefully, I dice the potatoes and toss the chunks into the pot, and then turn to watch Kaida as she points to each ingredient for the chocolate cake she plans to have ready for us after dinner. Kaida waves her hand around and pulls the ingredients to where she stands in front of a large mixing bowl. Even the three eggs are cracked perfectly without a single touch, not even the slightest sliver of shell.

Using one hand to animate the whisk, she points behind her with the other to bring a pan to the island in front of her. She finishes her spectacular show of magic by waving both hands together and opening the wood stove, sliding the pan in, and closing the door with two quick claps. Then, she whirls around in a circle and throws her hands into the air enthusiastically. "Ta-da! What do you think?"

My mouth might as well touch the floor as I stare at her in awe. Wordlessly, my eyes dart from her to the oven and back to her and it takes a moment for my brain to send the signal to my brain that I need to respond. "Kaida, that was absolutely miraculous. It was unlike anything you've ever done in front of me. How did you do that?"

Kaida looks at her feet sheepishly and shrugs. "I dunno. I just... did. My magic has grown over the last year or so, making it easier to use it for my baking without dropping anything or making any large messes. Now if I could only get it to wash the dishes. Then I'd really be impressed." The tinkling of her laughter bounces around the room as she carries the mixing bowl, measuring cups, and whisk to the sink. Waiting on the water to warm, she turns back toward me, her eyes twinkling. "Ellie, are you going to finish cooking our dinner? Asking because otherwise, you'll just stand there too long and we'll be eating scorched sausage and bread. Pick your chin up off the floor and get to it, Buttercup!"

I laugh, crossing the room and standing in front of the warm stove once more, adding cream cheese to the cooked sausage. Once the cheese melts, I dump a jarful of water on top to keep it from burning before adding in the potato chunks. Before long, I was filling bowls while Kaida slices into the fresh bread, the warm buttery scented steam rising from the now-broken crust.

Sitting on the sofa, side by side, we happily eat as we bask in the day's work. Though we hadn't been able to get much done, what we had managed to accomplish was enough to fill us with a sense of pride. The house settles into a sense of coziness as the sun sets, the crackling of burning wood in the fireplace setting up the perfect atmosphere that a cup of warm tea enhances. As the evening sky darkens with the blues of night, we struggle with staying awake, our eyes heavy with exhaustion. Staring into the flames in front of me, I can't stop the smile as it spreads across my face.

Maybe, just maybe, this is going to be the best change I have ever made.

The Farmer in the Dell

The next morning arrives entirely too fast. Cracking an eye open, I'm met with the unfortunate noise of a rooster's crow and the tips of the sun's rays as they peek over the horizon. She rolled over as she threw her blanket over her head and closed her eyes as tightly as possible. The crow of the rooster echoes across the farm again, a chorus of animals joining him as the donkey brays, Mabel neighs, pigs snort, and cows go "moo".

"I'm going to cook a rooster for dinner," I grumble under my breath as I stumble from the bed and reach for my robe. The relief the coziness grants me is only temporary, quickly replaced by the aching in my very full bladder that causes me to shuffle down the hallway at full speed.

Still rubbing the sleep from my eyes as I leave the bathing room, I head down the stairs where I set off into my morning routine; after I cut two slices of bread from the loaf, I scrape butter across the toast and this them into a cast-iron skillet on the stove until perfectly toasted. There's something about the act of continuing with my familiar motions that helps to ground me in the moment, which allows me to get more comfortable within my own body again.

I sigh with satisfaction as I smother the tops of my breakfast with apple jam, wasting no time before taking the first bite from the crisp toast. The crunch elicits a quiet, yet joyful noise that also announces the arrival of a still half-asleep Kaida, whom I look up to see as she shuffles into the kitchen, her palms rubbing the corners of her eyes. One glance at her still messy hair and the rumpled clothing she's still in from last night, and I know without a doubt that I wasn't the only one who's been ripped from sleep so rudely.

"Who decided that owning a rooster as a wakeup call was the best course of action to start the day?" Kaida asks, interrupted halfway through her question by a yawn that turns out to be infectious.

"I don't know, but I hope that they quickly regretted their poor decision. I tried to go back to sleep, but unfortunately, the rooster woke the other animals, too. So, I suppose today is our first day as farm girls, eh?" A nervous laugh bubbles from me before a sudden realization causes me to pause. "Erm... Have-have you ever... milked a cow?" I slowly ask.

Kaida lifts the kettle with a practiced smoothness, pouring the steaming water into both mugs without spilling a single drop before dunking a small muslin pouch of tea leaves into each. "Uh, I suppose it is, isn't it? And no. I haven't, Ellie. I'm guessing by the nervousness in your question that today will be the first time for you as well? Oh, well. Better to learn now. Hopefully, we won't be getting kicked in the head by some angry bovine," Kaida manages to say, despite the fit of giggles that erupts from her at what I can only assume to be the look of horror that spreads across my face.

We quickly drain our mugs and put them into the sink alongside our plates before racing upstairs to get dressed for the day. Once in the barn, I survey our surroundings, creating mental pictures of what equipment is located inside. On the wall, next to the rack of hay, is a nail that's holding up a milking pail that, being the braver of us, Kaida quickly grasps.

She waggles the fingers of her free hand at me as she saunters off in search of the cow, yelling that she will find me when she's done. Alone and unsure of what to do, I clumsily lift the pitchfork leaning next to the doorway and hoist a hay bale from the top of the rack. I wobble several times as I walk it to the stable next door, throwing it down for Mabel and the donkey.

With the weight no longer on the end, I walk briskly back to the barn and pick up a second bale to carry to the pig pen. This time, the weight leaves me wheezing after I throw it into the pig pen, trying to get it far enough from the muddy pit in the center that it doesn't get ruined before they can eat it.

As the pigs lazily drift over to inspect the gift, I attempt to stand straight, but end up placing my fisted hands over my hips as I try to get enough breath into me. Loudly, I huff and gasp, trying to fill my lungs as I rub my forehead across my lifted shoulder, desperately needing to wipe the sweat now rolling down my chin. I want to take a break before moving on to the chickens, but when I turn to the barn to put up the pitchfork, a shriek of terror echoes out from the direction Kaida had set out towards.

"I'm coming, Kai!" I scream, sprinting towards the sound. I've never been a fast runner, but knowing something could be wrong prompts my stubby legs to move as quickly as they can carry me.

It takes only seconds for me to reach her, but I'm still startled by the sight that greets me; Kaida is sitting in the center of the barn. In her lap is the now-empty pail, and milk drips from her hair and into her face. My face twists, and my brows knit in confusion as I stand inside the doorway. Before I can ask if she's okay, she laughs hysterically.

"What in the name of wild dragons is going on here, Kaida?!" I ask, trying to keep the annoyance from my voice.

With her hands clutching her sides, Kaida tries her hardest to explain what occurred in the moments before she screamed and why she's wearing more milk than is in the pail. It takes her several attempts, but finally, she's able to stop laughing just long enough for me to understand.

Taking a deep breath, Kaida launched into her explanation. "So, I went to milk the first cow, who I have named Bessie." She must see the look I give her because she pauses to explain. "I don't know why, but she looks like a Bessie to me. Don't judge me, Ellie. Anyways, I grabbed the pail and sat it under her so that her udders would be able to hover over it. Then, I grabbed two of them, one in each hand, and just kinda yanked. I got excited when I saw a stream leaking out from one of them, but I will have you know that I didn't squeal or shriek or yell a single time. And then I just kind of kept the same pace until it stopped, and none of the others had anything coming out either. Ellie, it was so cool! You should have been here! I still don't know how I did it, but whatever I did obviously worked." Her hands are waving wildly around her, the movements growing more erratic as she gets more excited.

"After I was sure she was empty, I moved the pail and stool over to where Brenda, the other cow, was standing and settled in to repeat the process I had done with Bessie. Something must have spooked her, though, because one moment I was sitting on the stool and the next I was on the ground with the empty pail in my lap. She must have kicked it over, dumping it out on me. As funny as I found it from my end, I can only imagine what it must have looked like from an outsider's point of view." She dissolves into another giggle fit, this time wheezing as she wipes tears from her eyes and milk off of her face while I stand speechlessly, massaging my temples with both hands.

After Kaida promises she's okay, I turn to leave. "I'm, uh, just gonna go handle the chickens. I'll meet you in the house for second breakfast."

She replies with a smile and a wave, telling me she'll see me after she showers. With one last look at my best friend, I shake my head as I walk to the chicken coop, mumbling under my breath that today can't get any more ridiculous. Thankfully, the chickens prove to be more successful for me than the cows did for Kaida, and I carry the basketful of eggs back to the house with me after feeding and watering the flock.

By the time I reach the kitchen and place the basket of eggs on the counter, Kaida has gotten the dining room table set. Plates, mugs, bread, cheese, strawberry jam, butter, and bacon cover the top, and my mouth waters at the thought of consuming so much delicious food. All of the work I've done today makes me hungry, and I rush to get enough eggs scrambled for the two of us.

While the eggs cook, I fill the kettle and place it on the stovetop so we can have a nice cuppa with our second breakfast.

"Ellie!" Kaida's squeal rings out from the den. "Those eggs smell delicious, especially with the scent of bacon filling the downstairs. Let's eat. I. Am. Starved."

We eat and eat, enjoying one another's company until we've eaten so much that we can hardly breathe. Between our full bellies and the energy we have spent already today, we wordlessly agree it's time for a well-deserved nap. I start the fire as Kaida pulls out the two coziest blankets from the linen closet, and, cuddled into the two oversized chairs, we quickly fall asleep.

The Gnome and the Grumpy Fae Next Door

By the time we wake, it's half past time for lunch, our nap consuming all of the time we would have spent on brunch and other busy work. After a light lunch, as we were both still fairly satisfied from our massive meal this morning, Kaida suggests we take some freshly baked treats to the neighbors on either side of us and introduce ourselves to our new neighbors. Cautiously, I agree, though nervousness settles inside of me like an unwelcome guest.

Hoping to distract myself, I pick the mystery novel I started reading last night and kick back in the chair while Kaida makes the baked goods—a mix of strawberry tartlets, lemon bars, and chocolate chip cookies. Time passes quickly as I become more absorbed in the story within my hands, and it seems like only moments pass before Kaida walks into the den with two expertly wrapped parcels.

As we approach the gate at the entrance, we look left and then right as we try to decide which neighbor to meet first. After a game of rock, paper, shears, it's decided that we should visit the neighbor on the left first. Though the house seems farther, it only takes us a dozen or so steps before we're standing on the doorstep of the dainty cottage.

The high roof is covered in moss mixed into other greenery, giving it an otherworldly appearance. It also doesn't appear to be bigger than an average-sized home, but rather one built for a family consisting of two or three beings. The yard is covered in wildflowers, not a single inch found without a flower bud, and the buzzing of bees can be heard from the road. Kaida knocks on the door and takes two steps back, stopping when she's back at my side, and we wait as an elderly female gnome opens the door.

She's fairly short, even by gnome standards, and has long, thin, pointed ears on either side of her aged, round face. Her long, graying hair has been intricately twisted into a braid before being wrapped into a bun that's secured at the top of her head by pins. The bright orange flowers woven through the coil catch my eye, and a vague flash of a memory of my grandmother pops into my mind.

Deep-set wrinkles surround her sparkling green eyes, suggesting that she's lived a full life that has heavily consisted mostly of smiling and happiness, while the tanned hue of her skin is evidence that she spends most of her time outside. She wears a modest yet beautiful green dress with a tea-stained, no-longer-white apron wrapped around her wide middle and a pair of worn, dark brown boots on her feet.

"May I help you?" she asks, the warmth in her smile radiating through her as she steps outside with us.

"Hullo," Kaida replies enthusiastically, smiling in return. "I'm Kaida, and this is Eilaen. We're your new neighbors and wanted to introduce ourselves."

Kaida extends one of the parcels to her, and she accepts it. "Thank you," she says, tucking the box under her arm. "I'm Lora Jean Kestrel." Her eyes find me, and a spark of recognition flashes within them, though she bites her lip as if uncertain of whether it would be polite to ask.

"You may have known my grandparents," I offer. "The Maplegrounds?"

The smile on her face spreads even further, the corners of her mouth practically reaching her ears. "Your grandmother was my closest and dearest friend. You must be Mason's daughter. I haven't seen you since you were knee-high and frolicking through the fields of the farm next door. Your laughter was beautifully infectious and echoed throughout the countryside. You were the apple of your grandfather's eyes, ya know. How's your father?"

"Oh, he passed away several years ago," I mumble, my eyes turning to the ground.

Whatever expression I wear must say more than I realize, because instead of asking more questions, she pats my arm empathetically. "I'm sorry, dearie. I lost touch with your grandfather after your grandmother passed away. It was around the same time that my Aldred passed, and I deeply regret not keeping in touch with him as much as I should have."

"I don't get many visitors these days as I'm typically the one doing the visiting," she tells us as she digs into the box to inspect its contents. "Unfortunately, this is one of those times. I desperately wish I could stay and chat, but I'm expected elsewhere. It was so lovely to meet you, Kaida and Eilaen, and I hope to see you again soon. Please feel free to pop by whenever you'd like." Placing the box on the ground, she wraps her arms around both of us in a grandmotherly gesture, one that hits deeper than I expect it to.

She releases us and picks up her package, a hum of pleasure rumbling from her as she plucks a chocolate chip cookie out of it. As we leave, we turn and wave just in time for her to smile behind the door now closing. By the time we reach the farm's gate, we hear the sound of her door as it opens and closes, and I'm surprised to note I'm comforted in knowing that she wasn't lying when she told us she couldn't stay. The sense of home and family I felt in the hug she gave us is one I haven't known in so long. It's also one I hope to feel again from her soon.

Hand in hand, Kaida and I continue until we reach the little house belonging to our neighbor on the right. As we approach the door, I stop at the bottom of the two-step rise while Kaida knocks. When nobody answers, Kaida's brows furrow deeply as we exchange uncertain glances before trading places. When I knock, she steps back, and from the corner of my eye, I watch as she rocks on her feet impatiently.

Light tapping startles me, and I jump as the noises on the other side of the door get louder, indicating that someone is actually inside. A loud thud sounds from inside the house, presumably from the other side of the door, and it jerks open just enough for us to see our neighbor's eyes. The rest of their face is covered with shadows, even with the sun trying to cut through the darkness spilling out of the cracked doorway.

"Whadduyou want?" The gruff voice sounds more annoyed than angry, but makes it clear that we're unwanted.

"Hullo. I'm Kaida, and this is Eilaen. We're your new neighbors! We just wanted to pop by for a moment so we could introduce ourselves. We came bearing gifts of freshly baked goodness!" Kaida's cheery voice matches her smile, and she wastes no time as she thrusts the bundle in her hand forward.

The door opens a fraction wider, and a Fae male appears in the crack. Though it's hard to be sure because the Fae age slowly compared to any other being, he looks to be close to our age. His round hazel eyes are topped with a pair of thick, dark eyebrows, and he has a mop of unruly, curly brown hair in desperate need of a brush and trim. His face, while not wholly unkind, is covered in a grumpy expression. The look he pins me with tells me he doesn't like that we're on his doorstep, and the way his eyes rake over us in disgust says more than his words probably would.

Then, he surprises me by moving outside, just outside the door, barely closing it behind him. I crane my neck to look up, annoyed to find he is incredibly tall compared to me, though this isn't anything new, as we halflings are well known for our short stature. The simple brown trousers are almost too short, skimming his ankles, and the loose orange shirt blows around him in the wind. When my eyes reach his face, I'm not surprised to see his face bear a frown. Mumbling a quick "thanks", he reaches out for the box Kaida is still extending to him. The moment he snatches it from her, he turns and barrels back into the house, slamming the door behind him. Before I have time to process what happened, the door opens again, and he's standing before us once more.

He folds his arms across his chest and speaks to us again, this time with a hard edge to his tone. "The name's Jareth. Leave me alone and don't bother me. We'll be just fine neighbors if you mind your own business." He pauses for a heartbeat before jerking his chin towards the farm. "If the garden starts to fall apart, leave a note on my door. I'll be over sometime that day to fix whatever you've messed up. You have the largest farm in the entire village, and it'll be of no use to anyone if it falls into ruin because two city-dwelling halflings took it upon themselves to take it over and immediately run it into the ground."

Without giving us time to say anything, he turns around and slams the door in our faces. Now alone, Kaida and I look at one another, gaping. I've never been spoken to by such a hateful, rude being, and the way he treated my best friend is appalling. His venom-laced words still ring in my ears as I attempt to process what has just transpired. How does one even respond to something like this?

Kaida's normally cheery face is crestfallen as we walk home, and Kaida rants about our rude neighbor and proclaims her wishes of how she hopes we never have to interact with him again. By the time we step through our door, she's finishing the slew of old elvish curses her granddad taught her when she was a small elfling. Her normally pink face is bright red, and her eyes are full of fury.

"C'mon Kaida. Let's go get cleaned up. Then, we can ride into town and check everything out," I suggest in a hopeful attempt to cheer her up.

With a sigh, Kaida gives me a reluctant nod. "Okay, Ellie. If you insist," she says, wiping her feet against the doormat and closing the door behind her.

An Unexpected Proposition

It takes time, but we settle down from our spat with the grump next door and the craziness from the morning enough to where we're confident enough to travel into town for the first time.

"I kind of know where we're going and where things are. But I have to be thereto tell you because we both know how my memory is," Kaida says.

Over the years, Kaida has made many trips to surrounding villages and towns for specialty baking ingredients, though Smallburrow has never been one she frequented. I think she's more excited to peruse the various stores than anything else she's done so far today whereas I'm more than ecstatic that the farm resides on the outskirts of the town, so while the distance makes it too far to walk, it's still within a comfortable riding distance without the wagon, especially if we decide to make any purchase.

As Mable and the donkey, lovingly named Sorel by Kaida, leisurely trot down the bumpy dirt road, Kaida and I fall into our usual pattern of her chattering nonstop while I comment in between her sporadic breaths. It doesn't take long, however, before the road transitions from the loose, dusty stones into the tightly packed cobblestone announcing we've reached the town proper.

"Maybe while we're here today we can find a location for the new bakery! How wonderful would it be to have two storefronts of my very own?" Kaida sighs dreamily, and I swear I see the swirling of magic within her eyes.

I hum in agreement before the urge to retreat into myself rises in me. There has never been, nor will there ever be, a time when I haven't willingly and enthusiastically supported Kaida in her dreams. She's my best friend and the closest thing I've ever had to a sister. But there have been many times when I have had the desire to possess the same ambition and drive Kaida has when she decides to push for whatever goal she settles on.

With a sigh, I think about the single dream I've kept in my heart for as long as I can remember. It's one I've never spoken about out loud; not even to Kaida. Since I was little, I've dreamed of owning and running a farm like my grandparents. Not only do I want my farm to be successful, but I long to have one that is beneficial to the entire town's needs. Now that we live on a farm so much like the one of my dreams, I can finally allow myself to see if I can make the dream come true. I just have to find a way to believe that I can take Mapleground Farm and mold it into the farm of my dreams.

I open my mouth to start the discussion, but Market District appears before us before I find the words to say, Kaida's squeals of excitement interrupting my thoughts. I dismount Mable when we reach the gate and, after Kaida dismounts Sorrel and ties her up, we look around the scene before us. I take it all in, my hands spread over the wide expanse of my hips, as the chaos of the market district unfolds before me. Surprisingly, there are quite a number of—what I assume to be—townsfolk littering the streets and sidewalks. My astonishment only grows whenever we walk through the gates of the market and I see the vast array of booths and merchants it contains.

The first book is empty, no signs of an occupant anywhere to be seen. Two booths down from that sit an elderly goblin couple selling fish by the pound. An unmanned booth several steps down from them has foraged goods, though I don't see the merchant anywhere around. The assortment of unique wares catch my eye, but I guess I'll have to find them later to make a purchase.

Kaida and I exchange several glances as we continue weaving through the maze of people and goods. One person is selling custom dyed rolls of cloth, while the merchant to their right has fresh goat cheese and large pitchers of goat milk. Down another row, a dwarvish merchant expertly haggles with the one next to them, the two dwarves trying to come to an agreement of metal bars per gemstones.

"That dwarf has smelted the metal bars made from iron, gold, copper, and iridium. All by hand! It takes five ore per bar to have enough when melted down. It's truly a work of art." Her voice holds reverence for the dwarf at the craftsmanship that was put into the items in front of him.

What other treasures could be hidden deep in this overwhelming sea of trinkets and edibles around me?

Though amazing, the experience I've been surrounded by is overwhelming and has me wanting to hide somewhere small and quiet. I can't help but notice that there's something lacking, even with everything else here. The knot between Kaida's brows tells me she also notices that something is off.

"Have you noticed what I have?" she whispers, leaning her head close enough to mine that I can hear her over the noise.

I nod. "No vegetables. No fruit. No bread," I reply.

"Exactly!" Her hands fly up. "No bread. No muffins or pies or cookies to be found. Not even the crumbs from a small cake!" Her exasperation is noticed by several people around us, but I don't think they heard what she said.

The realization lights the small spark of hope living next to my dream, and I bite my lip in anticipation of discussing it with Kaida. But it's definitely time for me to share it with her. Her support will be monumental in whatever small amounts of success I may experience, and there's nobody else that I'd rather have at my side.

Finally, we've finish the loop through the district and find ourselves at the entrance once again. Before we can cross through the gate, Ms. Kestrel cries out for us.

Waving enthusiastically, she calls to us. "Yoohoo! How wonderful it is to run into you two again. You're just the two halflings I was hoping I would run into," she says with a large smile. Beside her stands a beautiful orcess who is also smiling at us, nodding her head in a greeting as we walk to them.

Grabbing one of our hands within hers, Ms. Kestrel introduces us to the orcess, who then introduces herself. "Good afternoon. I'm Urzal, head of the Market District council, as well as the mayor's wife. Pleased to make your acquaintance."

Kaida enthusiastically reaches for Urzal's hand and shakes it vigorously. "Hullo! I'm Kaida and this is Eilaen. We're the new residents over at the Mapleground Farm, just outside of town. Grandfather Mapleground was her granddad, ya see. He left it to her when he passed." Kaida said as she introduces me, barely taking a breath before spilling into a proposition. "By the by, we're loving the market. However, we couldn't help but notice you're missing a thing or two from your collection."

Urzal lifts a perfectly manicured eyebrow at this. "Is that so?" she asks, the corner of her mouth tilting upwards at Kai's forwardness.

"Indeed it is," Kaida continues. "As we walked through the entirety of this District, I was rather disappointed when I didn't see a single merchant who had any produce or baked goods. It had me wondering: is this something you're in need of to round out the market?"

With an amused expression, Urzal nods. "You are correct, Kaida. Ms. Kestrel was actually just telling me how delicious the tartlets you brought her were. I knew that Mr. and Mrs. Mapleground had an estranged granddaughter, but I didn't know who she was. I'm very pleased to meet the both of you. Since you're here, may I be the first to welcome you officially to Smallburrow, as well as extend an invitation to join the market as a merchant?" She asks, patiently waiting for our reply.

"We would absolutely love to join the market!" I hear myself exclaim, though I'm not sure when I decided I would speak. I typically leave that part to Kaida as she can typically express herself better than I can. As if hearing my thoughts, Kaida turns to me, her sparkling green eyes wide with surprise. Nervously, I clear my throat and then continue speaking. "I mean, what I meant to say was that we would love to discuss renting a booth and selling our baked treats and produce. Right, Kaida?"

A large smile stretches across Kaida's face, and the sparkle in her eyes gets even brighter. "Of course! When can we discuss details?" Kaida replies, turning back towards Urzal.

I sigh in relief as the nerves fluttering inside of me settle.

The next thought makes me smile. This is really happening. Unfortunately, the familiar sensation of panic appears and as it attempts to weigh down my chest, I take several deep, slow breaths to push it away. This is going to happen and I resolve to refuse to allow myself to get in the way of my dream.

By this time next year, the farm will prove to be a success, one way or another, I promise myself, ignoring the doubts now swirling inside of my head. We spend the rest of the afternoon discussing the necessary details regarding payments, booth location, and market dates. A new sense of purpose washes over me as we leave the orcess' office. Two days a week, we will be setting up at the booth closest to the entrance, the empty one we saw two booths away from the fish selling goblins. An exchanged look between the two of us reveal that we both agree—the fishy smell would be more than worth it if it means we can provide Smallburrow with the things we have to offer.

We wave goodbye to Urzal and Ms. Kestrel as we leave the market district, chatting excitedly as we untie the horse and donkey that have been patiently waiting on us. As we start out on our way home, Kaida turns to me, peering at me with curiosity. Seeing her from the corner of my eye, I raise an eyebrow before looking at my friend. "What's on your mind, Kai?"

"Oh, nothing at all. Just, ya know, wondering when you grew so bold as to speak so openly to a complete stranger. That's all." Kaida's shoulders lift and fall nonchalantly.

I laugh, knowing she's been itching to ask for awhile now. "I have to admit. I surprised myself. I'd like to say that you've finally rubbed off on me after all of these years, but I think we both know that isn't the truth." I pause, taking a deep breath and deciding to push through. I need to tell her.

"Actually, there's something I need to tell you that I haven't ever told anyone. It seems silly, actually, but for as long as I can remember, I have always wanted a farm of my own. One that I can use to help whatever town I lived in and the people who lived there too. You know, kind of like a "see a need, fill a need" kind of thing? When I saw the chance for me to take Mapleground Farm and create something beautiful and needed with it, I couldn't help but jump at the opportunity." A hesitant sigh flows through me, coming from somewhere deep within me after I speak.

Kaida stops talking, her face visibly showing her processing my confession. "Well, Ellie," she says slowly. "If that's your dream, then I'm gonna make sure you live it. We'll do whatever it takes to make it come true. Just watch! I don't care what I have to do to help you see your dream come to life like you've helped me with mine. We'll figure this out together, just like always." She reaches across the space between us and takes my hand before squeezing it.

Her support means more to me than she will ever know. I honestly don't remember a time when I haven't been thankful to know and love Kaida, her friendship a gift I have never deserved. If it wasn't for Kaida and her insistance, I'd still be in Galbassi, never having been brave enough to come to Smallburrow and my dream would forever be out of reach.

Smiles plastered on our faces, we ride the remainder of the distance home, chattering excitedly about everything we need to do before our market debut, which is less than a week away. Tomorrow, I'll need to figure out all of the necessary logistics regarding my half of the market deal. Tonight, though? Tonight, I refuse to do anything but ride the high that only comes with the realization that the path to one's dream is finally within their grasp.

We're starving when we get home and, as I tend to Mable and Sorrel, Kaida whips up a simple dinner of cucumber sandwiches and the remaining tartlets from this morning. We sit in silence as we eat, still reeling from the excitement of the day. From spooked cows to grumpy neighbors to living out our dreams, I think the reality that our adventure has only just begun finally sinks in.

The rest of the evening drifts by far too quickly, moving as if time was nothing more than a blink of an eye. When the clock chimes the sound of ten o'clock, we bid one another a goodnight. I drain the remainder of tea in my cup and listen to the fire crackle and the sounds of Kaida's footsteps on the stairs, heading to bed once my cup is in the sink.

As I settle down into bed, I realize I haven't quit smiling all evening, the expression still plastered on my face as my eyes get heavy. Sleep claims me almost instantaneously as I pull my blanket up over my shoulders, barely taking a breath before I slip into a deep sleep where cows throw pails of milk around and roosters cry "moo".

Seize the Pig (or Whatever They Say)

It takes ages to get moving, weariness weighing on my limbs as if there were a basket of iron ore on each of them, and I have to coerce myself to walk outside. As I drag along, I think of the changes and challenges we've already faced, as well as the potential for those to come. In the week since signing the documents that will allow Kaida and I to rent our booth in Market District, I've been forced to learn a lot more than I could have foreseen.

Like, for instance, that I have to eat before tending to the farm, especially if I want to avoid creating a scene from getting hangry. It's been two days since learning this, and I still have to fight the urge to apologize to Kaida this morning as I jam my wide feet into my boots.

It takes ages to get moving, weariness weighing on my limbs as if there were a basket of iron ore on each of them, and I have to coerce myself to walk outside. To my surprise, Tillard's face is there to greet me as he stands in the middle of the field that separates the backyard from the farm animals' grazing areas. A shiver runs down my spine at the mischievous smirk he gives me—I didn't even know pigs could smirk—and I brace myself for the impending chase I know is coming.

His eyes never leave mine, and he watches intently as I crouch, squealing when I leap towards him. I almost catch him, but as soon as my fingers graze the side of his neck, he bolts in the opposite direction. He runs faster than I do, bobbing and weaving, his hooves launching clods of dirt in every direction.

Something burns in my chest and whether it's frustration or my lungs gasping for air, I'm not sure. Either way, it doesn't take much longer for me to stop, bending at the waist with my hands grasping my knees as I try to catch my breath. As if I didn't already have enough of a reason to despise the meathead without the two of us going round and round in circles, the memory of waking up last week to find him snoring on the couch in the den pops into my mind and my anger only bubbles closer to the surface. My lips pull downwards into a frown, the expression deepening as I watch him prance into the pig pen, keeping a steady pace as he passes me.

This time, I can't hold back a growl and it rumbles through me. My trousers stick to me uncomfortably, and I look down to find that mud cakes them, starting just under my knees and encasing the entirety of my legs and boots. *After chores, I'm going to sit in the wash tub and just relax*, I promise myself as I continue towards the barn.

My resolve sticking to me as firmly as the leg of my trouser, I turn my thoughts to the task at hand and grab the pail off the wall. As I slide the pail underneath Bessie and milk her, my mind starts flipping through the logistics that come with selling produce to the townsfolk at the market. There is still so much for me to learn in regards to farming and animal husbandry, yet not enough time.

Where do I start? Forget where, I don't even know how to dive into this. I groan and immediately feel the warmth of Bessie's breath as she huffs, almost as if with me. I should have done more to prepare before now, I should have gone into town and looked through the books in the library, asked around, anything. But did I? No, no I did not. Instead, I've stayed here where it was comfortable and safe, where it was familiar, and ducked my head into the sand like an ostrich hiding.

My party-of-one self-pity party continues as my thoughts continue to spiral until I remember the entire wall of books inside the study; the door hasn't even been opened since the initial visit to the farm and that was almost a month ago. The epiphany hits me as I wrap up with milking Brenda, and I leave the barn smiling. *All I need to do is buckle down and read. I can do that.*

Easy peasy, lemon squeezy.

My sudden burst of inspiration spurs me into action and I work fast until my work is done. Kaida's eyes grow wide as she looks at me, but she doesn't say a word, probably having heard the morning's commotion through the kitchen window. Instead, she silently hands me a fresh cream cheese danish and a cup of cold milk, and I devour it before climbing into the tub in desperation of removing the filth from my body.

Belly full and no longer looking like Tillard's twin, I slip into the study, slowly inspecting it once again. As before, the scent of the past greets me in the form of old book pages, ink, leather, and parchment sweep across the room. The thick tomes before me beckon for my attention, and I have to carefully read the titles to avoid getting sucked into their details like I'm apt to do. Relief fills me when I realize the titles lining the wall were left in order, first being organized by subject and then by title.

My fingers trail across the spines of the garden books, the spring greens and bright yellows pleasing to look at, and when I locate one titled *Gardening for Beginners*, I pull it from the shelf. With the thick volume in hand, I step across the room and gently sit at the desk, the plush cushion in the chair more comfortable than it looks. Dust particles fill the air before tickling my nose, a sneeze building inside for a moment before settling down. In an attempt to maximize my productivity, I open the book and surround it with the ink, quills, and parchment stacked in one corner, hoping that I'll remember to take notes as I read.

Time ceases to exist as I become immersed in the information before me, my greedy brain sucking it down as quickly as possible. The ink staining my skin goes unnoticed and it isn't until my stomach makes loud noises that I look up, surprised to see how long I've been reading. The sky outside has been painted by the sun, the vast array of oranges and purples blending into one another as day turns to night. With a large yawn, I shake my hands to relieve the cramping in my fingers and glance over to find the clock on the wall, shocked to find it's already past suppertime.

The day is completely gone, and I have no idea how the afternoon managed to slip away so quickly, nor can I recall the last time I was so engrossed in my studies that time might as well have meant nothing. I pop the quill into the ink pot and stand, keeping place in the book with my notes. I need to invest in a better bookmark, I muse as I rise to my feet, hoping the ink has dried completely and won't transfer from parchment to book pages.

Rubbing the palm of one hand with the fingers of the other, I slowly shuffle into the kitchen and mentally beg the stiffness in my body to dissolve. Wonder if Kaida whipped something up, I think, not expecting the movement on the other side of the doorway to prompt my steps to halt. Taking note of Kaida's carefree expression and the sheer fluidity of her movements, I dare not make a single peep or risk distracting her.

There's nothing in this world that embodies magic quite like Kaida when she's experimenting with new baking techniques and creations. Kaida has always been the embodiment of magic as she experiments with a new baking creation. Half of the experience in watching her is how gracefully Kaida moves, so wholly in her own world and element, creating a picture of sorts. She's a work of art, waltzing across the kitchen as if she's rehearsing a dance of her own creation, her chosen ingredients moving around as if they have been choreographed to do so. I wait to announce my presence until both the flour and the bowl of egg yolks have deposited themselves into the large mixing bowl on the island's counter top, clearing my throat to do so.

Turning long enough to greet me with a smile, she then dives hand first into the mixture she's conjured. Her breathing is even and there is no sense of impatience or rush as she mashes it together, kneading it to perfection. Subtle hints of brown sugar and chocolate fill the space between us, and I smile. The moment is too much like the first time I asked her what her magic felt like when baking, and her answer has stuck with me for the entirety of our friendship.

"It feels as if my hands are at home when they're caked in dough. My mind is empty. Nothing exists, no thoughts run amuck. It's the only time I feel as if I can truly just be. It's as if the magic takes a piece of me and a piece of whatever it is I'm baking, melding the pieces together until it's seamlessly been blended into one entity."

Maybe I can experience that feeling one day, my mind whispers to my heart, and in this moment, I wish for nothing more than to feel the same as she does with my hands, dirt caked under my nails, as I nurture plants to life. My thoughts consume me, distracting me as I mindlessly go through the motions and set the kettle on the stove for a hot cup of tea. Blinking rapidly, I pull myself out of it and turn towards her. "Kai? Tomorrow is our first market day, huh?"

Kaida looks up, nodding enthusiastically as she forms a ball with the dough in her hands. "It is and I am so excited!" The last word in her sentance is more song than spoken word, and is followed by a small chuckle. "What about you? Are you ready?"

I grimace at her question. "Well…" I trail off, not knowing how to explain my anxious thoughts or the doubts plaguing me.

"So, you haven't harvested anything you're planning on taking then?" Her brow quirks up into an arch and she blinks slowly.

"Erm, I… have not," I admit, biting my lip.

She shakes her head lightheartedly. "Then you best get your hiney out there and get some veggies plucked."

Now it's my turn to raise a brow. "Pluck the veggies, Kai?"

"What do you expect from me? I'm a baker, not a farmer. When was the last time I tried to grow anything? Hmm?" When I stay silent, she clears her throat and a glint of mischief sparkles in her emerald colored eyes. "Yeah, that's what I thought. If it makes you feel better, then I'll admit that it… Beets me!"

"Kaida Louise," I groan, my hands flying to my face as I shake my head.

Her cackle fills the room. "Get it? Beets me? Because beets are a vegetable!" Her entire body shakes as she laughs, her breaths turning into gasps.

"Yeah, I get it. You're so punny," I remark with a smile. "Guess I'll go work on that."

Turning around, I let Kaida know that I'll be outside if she needs me and grab the basket from its resting hook next to the front door.. Guilt rushes through me when I consider that I'm in the grey area where my lack of admission could have been a lie. Maybe I should have admitted to her that harvesting produce has been the last thing on my mind and that I have been far too focused on learning how to grow the plants. So much so that tonight also happens to be the first time I've realized just how unbothered I have been with that side of the operation.

Feet planted firmly into the ground, I assess the garden before me as I clutch my chin in my hand. With a quick glance, I'm almost certain that the corn is ready. The plot next to my feet contains tomatoes, cucumbers, and snap peas that also appear to be ripe enough for harvesting. I move further into the field, looking over each section meticulously. Based on what I read earlier, I'm fairly confident the cauliflower, beets, elephant garlic, and cabbage need a little more time to grow, and I make the snap decision to save those for another day.

When it comes to whether or not the potatoes, onions, and carrots are ready, I'm less sure, ultimately leaving them be for next week, just in case the ones I previously grabbed ended up being anomalies. Finished with the vegetables, I make my way towards the fruit bushes and trees, knowing most items are probably already too far gone to be worth anything but animal chow. By the time I'm done with my trek through the garden, I'm surprised to find I've managed to acquire four full baskets of vegetables, berries, and herbs.

Once my haul has been unloaded onto the dining room table and Kaida whistles her approval, we sort through everything piece by piece and divide the goods between what we plan to keep for our personal use and the prettier produce that should sell nicely tomorrow. The more we sort, the more we marvel at the size and variety in front of us.

By the time we finish, we have successfully divided everything into two equal piles, and for the first time all day, I don't feel the sensation of dread sitting in my gut. Instead, excitement replaces it, and I have to keep myself from bouncing with joy, choosing instead to tap my fingers together in rhythm at my side. had been divided into half. Before stopping for the night, we go over the items Kaida has baked this week, taking stock of everything. In the end, we log eight fully stuffed parcels filled to the brim with baked goods, as well as six loaves of bread and twelve different fruit pies.

Together, we load our arms with the items we decided to keep and lug them into the kitchen, both realizing how hungry we are now that our arms are empty and our minds aren't busy. "I'll make something for supper," I tell her, guiding her towards the dining room. "You go into the den and relax. You look tired."

She agrees, but not before scrunching her nose at me and stocking out her tongue in mock protest. Alone, I look around and pick up several small vegetables, two potatoes, a handful of carrots that she'd harvested the day before, and a medium hunk of lamb. After peeling and dicing the potatoes, I plop them into a pot of boiling water with butter, salt, and pepper. Next, I pick up my favorite cast iron skillet and it makes a metallic thunk as I put it on top of the wood stove.

Once it's heated, I melt two large scoops of garlic-infused butter in it before gently placing the lamb hunk inside to sear. The mouth watering aroma of the butter quickly follows the satisfying sizzle of the meat as it cooks, keeping the lamb in the skillet only long enough to sear it on all sides before moving it to the wooden cutting board beside me to rest. While waiting, I dice the carrots and onion I selected and toss them into a large bowl, shelling two dozen or so peas to add to them.

By this time, the potatoes have boiled and are ready to be drained and mashed, I've finished slicing the lamb into small pieces, as well as creating gravy from the juices left in the pan from it cooking and stirring the meat bits into it. Finally, I mash the potatoes, and then assemble the casserole; on the bottom, I spread the vegetable mixture, pouring the lamb and gravy in the dish to make the middle layer. The top layer is finished off with the potato mash that I add crumbled cheese onto before popping into the oven, the blazing heat almost setting my eyebrows on fire.

"Ellie, do I smell burnt hair?" Kaida calls from the den, doing nothing but increasing my panic regarding the oven door.

"No," I yell, hoping she can hear me over the squeak of the

rusty hinges that keep the oven's door firmly attached to the wooden stove.

Small aches and pains work through my muscles, the day's work finally catching up with me. Even still, I find myself happy with everything I've done, smiling to myself as I clean the kitchen while waiting for supper to finish. My timing is perfect, and the final dish goes into the drainer when the glorious scent of shepherd's pie overtakes my senses. It must be just as enticing to Kaida, because she skips into the kitchen claiming to be ravenous and on the brink of starvation. Together, we work side by side as I dish out the food and she pours each of us a drink. To celebrate the success of our first week of living in Smallburrow, we clink our glasses against one another and cry out "cheers!".

We waste no time devouring our food, and I laugh when I see Kaida wiggling around as she dances happily while moaning about the food touching her soul.

"Ellie, if you weren't already trying your hardest on your farming dream, I'd insist that you open up a restaurant with me. This is the most delicious thing I've ever eaten!" She sighs contentedly before adding, "I'm going to gain so much weight with you cooking for me every night." She makes a happy noise as she takes another bite, dramatically rolling her eyes into the back of her head.

We chat as we eat, commenting on topics ranging from our smallest hopes to our largest dreams, all connected to the wishes we have for our new life in Smallburrow. By the time we finish our after-supper clean up, we've danced and sang the night away and are both ready to settle down in our beds and sleep.

As I drift off to sleep, excitement courses through me at what tomorrow can bring and I cannot wait to experience our first day in Number One Booth. All of my dreams are decorated with visions of the sights and sounds of the market, and even as I sleep, I know that this can be nothing less than the start of something wonderful and what I hope will only be described as my dream come true.

These Little Halflings Went to the Market

Morning arrives quickly, and for once, I'm excited for the day rather than dragging as I wake up. In a hurry, I dress warmly and sprint down the stairs, stopping in the kitchen to fill the kettle and set it on the stove, and then yell to Kaida that she needs to wake up. I don't bother waiting for a response other than the groan of displeasure she gives me before bolting outside and dashing towards the animals. In record speed, I collect the eggs from the chickens and milk both Brenda and Bessie before hurrying back towards the house to pack the wagon with produce.

Not even Tillard, who stands in the field between the barn and the garden, can ruin my mood today. Thankfully, he doesn't put up much of a fight before choosing to saunter towards his pen as I march towards him. Relief washes over me, and my muscles loosen when I realize he has no wish to fight me today, allowing me to continue on my mission as quickly as planned. Passing the garden and vegetables I chose to leave unharvested, I give it a quick passing glance as I travel the final steps towards the house.

I'll look everything over whenever we get home this afternoon, I promise myself as I pass by the plots. From the stable, Mable whinnies, reminding me that I need to get her and the wagon moved in front of the farmhouse so Kaida and I can load up our market wares, causing me to spin around and march across the field once again.

Just as I pull up in front of the door, Kaida steps outside

with arms overflowing from all of the baked treats she'd gathered while waiting for me to come back inside. As she carefully packs and arranges the baked goods into the wagon, I step around her and go into the house, a chill spreading through me as the warmth sinks through my skin. Once inside, I notice how the delicious aroma of the fresh mixed berry tarts mingles with the earthy scent of this morning's tea, and it reminds my stomach that I have yet to eat. As it rumbles, I walk further into the house, reaching the doorway of the kitchen when I hear Kaida's voice.

"I left a warm tart and your tea on the island for you, Ellie! Stuff it down and let's get this show on the road," her voice calls out, immediately followed by her "oomph" as the door audibly hits her.

With a happy dance, I eat as quickly as possible while also taking large mouthfuls of tea between each bite. Cup empty and belly full, I hurriedly make my way to the produce and grab as much as I can at once before taking it to the wagon. Three armfuls later, I've gotten everything we plan to take outside while Kaida arranges and rearranges it in the back of the wagon, taking care to ensure none of the fragile produce bruises or pies break in the process. Happy with what we've selected, we give each other a large smile before scrambling into the wagon seat and setting off, our excited chattering filling the space around us.

The sounds of overlapping voices reach us before we pull to a stop, the market already busy and overflowing with vendors as they set up for the day. The flurry of movement is nothing short of overwhelming as we load our arms and make our way to Number One Booth.

Seeing my discomfort, Kaida looks at me and lays her hand on my elbow. "Ellie, why don't you finish bringing everything in while I work on getting it all set out and organized? Two birds, one stone, right?" Her gentle smile radiates love and kindness, reminding me that I'm not alone today. Nodding, I force myself to take a slow breath and then return to the wagon.

It takes several trips before the wagon is empty, and the

first customers are entering the gates as I sit next to Kaida. Moments later, we're up and ready for the townsfolk to stop by. The first several hours pass in a blur of exchanging produce for coins, the exchange occurring more frequently than I could have prepared myself for.

Finally, it's time to take a break and stretch our legs. After Kaida places a sign on our table stating we'll be back soon, we decide to take a lap around the market to see what others have to offer today. Before we can finish rounding the table, however, Ms. Kestrel spies us and shuffles over to us with an enthusiastic wave that I've contributed to the elderly gnome as part of her usual greeting.

"Good mornin', girls! How is everything going today?" She asks as she stops in front of us. Without waiting for our answer, she continues speaking. "You girls look tired and as if you're taking a break? That's perfect timing on my part. Come along, I have some folks I'd like to introduce to you that weren't here last week."

Grasping us both by the hand with a surprising amount of strength, Ms. Kestrel drags us behind her until we reach the halfway point of the market before stopping. In that grandmotherly way of hers, she smiles at the orc she's stopped in front of, nodding her head. "Girls, this is Mayor Luddie. Mayor Luddie, this is Kaida and Eilaen. They're the new residents at Mapleground Farm."

I take a moment to examine the mayor, surprised to see that the orc before us is very well put together, unlike the nonsense spewed by the Galbassi Gossip Network, the unofficial name for the group of old biddies that would sit in Kaida's Bakery back home and do nothing but sip their tea and gossip all day. Mayor Luddie, chatting animatedly to Kaida, is the opposite of brutish and ugly.

His friendly face rivals Kaida's as the friendliest face I've seen on another person, and his light green skin is almost glowing in the sunlight. His long tusks are well-manicured, and his clothing wrinkle-free and well-pressed. His large, toothy smile stretches across his face, and his eyes, though staring at me intently, hold nothing but kindness. His hairline appears to be in the earlier stages of receding, though it's not unbecoming on him.

"Good morning," his deep, warm voice booms. "As Ms. Kestrel has already said, I'm Mayor Luddie. I've heard a little bit about you two from my wife, Urzal. She seems to be rather fond of you both already."

"Pleasure to meet you," I squeak as Kaida extends her hand towards him.

His attention turns towards the elderly gnome beside us. "Don't forget, Ms. Kestrel. You've promised Urzal and me that you'll be at our house for supper tomorrow evening. We're looking forward to it."

She scoffs playfully, swatting at his arm. "I may be old, but I'm not that old, Luddie boy. I will be there, bells and whistles and all."

Before he can reply, Urzal appears at his side and leans in to whisper something into his ear. His expression transforms from jovial to stoic, his features growing harder before he nods at her, excusing himself from the conversation. The orcess smiles, acknowledging Kaida, Ms. Kestrel, and me before following her husband, the two of them whispering as they walk away quickly.

Though Ms. Kestrel has already introduced us to the majority of the townsfolk, she still drags us across the market to greet friends of hers and make our acquaintance with those we haven't met yet. After a while, there are so many names that they all spin in my head and I can no longer distinguish the founding ogre families from those of the traveling orcs at the end of the market. Kaida, picking up on my distress once again, comes to my rescue and tells Ms. Kestrel that we need to return to our booth. Bidding her goodbye, we invite her to dinner later this week, and she enthusiastically accepts, promising to come by in the next day or so to discuss details.

The elderly goblins in the booth next to us, Jax and Keshi, strike up a conversation about their love for bartering. By the time they walk over to their own booth, we've swapped two pies and a basket of produce for three massive tunas and a small basket of oysters. We also learn during our conversation with them that they have both been residents of Smallburrow for both of their lives, as well as the name of the merchant who runs

Number Five Booth—a forager gnome that goes by the name Nadles and is known for the exotic and enchanted foragables that she sources from forests all around the world.

Things slowly settle down as an afternoon lull hits the market, giving us time to breathe and reflect on our day thus far, the stillness alerting me to Jareth's presence as he walks through the market's entrance. He walks by us strangely, not bothering to throw us a glance as he gives Number One Booth a wider-than-necessary berth before continuing down the row of merchants. The grumpy Fae continues to catch my attention when he steps into my peripheral vision, and I watch him turn and come closer as if wanting to come to us. Each time, he stops halfway and turns around.

In the span of a week, his hair has become closer to an unruly mop, now donning chocolate brown ringlets on the ends. His bright green eyes sparkle when he laughs, which happens frequently as he stops to talk to the other townsfolk, his narrow nose crinkling when doing so. It doesn't escape my notice that, as time passes and the lull continues, I catch myself staring at him. He's become a person of interest rather than just the rude Fae boy who lives next door to my farm, and I now want to know why he was so rude to us last week.

It's on his third lap around the market, and the unexpected happens. Instead of passing by us as if we're invisible or turning before reaching the halfway mark of where he is and where we are, he stops at Number One Booth and looks through the items we have left, which isn't much, as we're at the end of the day.

His brow furrows at our selection, and I bite my tongue instead of telling him that we would have had more if he had stopped by one of the dozens of other times he walked towards us. Thankfully, Kaida has no reservations about helping him, which he must sense because he directs his attention to her when he clears his throat. "Is- is there any way that I could, uhm, place an order? You know, for pickup?"

She nods with a smile, reaching over to grab a scrap of paper and a wooden pencil, writing down his order and asking questions about his preferences as he speaks. By the time Kaida pockets the slip of paper, he's ordered two loaves of sweet bread, two pumpkin pies, and a dozen lemon raspberry tartlets for pick up on the first market day of next week. Before placing the coins on the table, his hand hovers over the table before he points to the final basket of assorted vegetables and asks to purchase them, as well.

Basket in hand, he promises to return the basket and mumbles a quick "thank you" as he drops his eyes to the ground and slides the coins towards Kaida and me. He doesn't give us time to say "have a great day" before shuffling out of the market with his eyes still cast downward.

"Well, that was rather, uhm, interesting," I say after a moment, breaking the silence that has settled over us. "Did you notice the lack of apology or even an acknowledgment of how he'd treated us last week?"

"That's exactly what I was thinking. He's an odd duck, isn't he? And you already know that I did notice that. I almost said something, too. The only reason I didn't is that I didn't want to be overly dramatic and end up causing a scene in the middle of our first day as merchants of Number One Booth. But now I'm wondering why he hasn't just popped over to the farm to make an order, especially since he went through so much trouble to do so in public. According to her, you can smell it way over at Ms. Kestrel's house when I'm baking something, so I don't think it would be too far to say he must be able to smell it over at his house, too. Poor guy must have gone back and forth almost two dozen times before finally gathering the gumption to come over and talk to us." She laughs.

"Did you know that Ms. Kestrel has told me more than once that she has to hold herself back so she'll resist showing up at our door before the sun rises? She would absolutely adore getting her hands on a hot cake or a lemon tart when they're fresh from the oven."

As we wait to pack up, I sit and contemplate Jareth's actions. It perplexes me how vastly different the two interactions I've had with him have been, and I'm unable to make sense of it. Shaking my head, I try to focus on what the next person says as they talk about prices and place an order with Kaida, whose laugh rings out as she counts out change for the customer.

I breathe, relieved to see my expectations haven't been set too high as we pack up our things moments later. Kaida's entire stock sold, and mine isn't far behind; the only things I have left are a couple of ugly tomatoes that have bruised and a carrot that has a wilted stem. Knowing we're still setting first impressions and our reputation as merchants, I'm pleasantly surprised with how well we've done today, and my heart soars.

This is how my dream begins, I tell myself as I place an armful of baskets in the wagon. Though it's still likely, maybe I won't have to dip into the reserves Grandfather Mapleground left me in the bank to care for the farm with, and we can be financially stable, even through the winter.

Even with how great today has been, my mood plummets as we finish packing everything up, the need to shut my brain off, and without pretending to be happy and outgoing, growing quicker as each moment passes. All I want to do now is to get home, make a cuppa, and cuddle up with my book. I need to do a little more than simply exist for a little while and reset. Thankfully, our home seems to take half the amount of time than it did this morning, and we pull into the yard silent and exhausted.

I let Kaida jump out of the wagon and collect the baskets before pulling Mable and the wagon out to the back so I can tend to her needs before taking care of my own. I give her a generous rub down and an extra helping of food, turning away as I pat her haunches.

I'm so tired that I don't even think about checking the garden as I had planned to this morning. Instead, I walk through the front door and close it before climbing the stairs to soak in the tub. Any previous thoughts of tending the still unharvested produce are completely forgotten, my brain in a post-social interaction fog.

The soak in the tub does exactly what I had hoped it would do, my aching muscles and tired mind relaxing more by the second. I travel down the stairs with stubby fingers and toes that resemble prunes more than the digits they were when I climbed into the hot water. Now it's time to sit by the fire and get cozy with my book, a plush blanket, and a nice cup of tea. We've been so busy the last several weeks that I haven't had much of a chance to just be, and I desperately need the soul-refreshing rejuvenation it gives.

From the corner of my eye, I see Kaida as she walks out of the den when I reach the bottom step, her footsteps moving towards the kitchen as mine head towards my favorite chair. When I round the sofa, I'm touched by Kaida's kindness at the sight of a steaming cup of tea and a fresh cream cheese scone next to my mystery book, the items sitting on the end table next to my chosen seat. Maybe it's from being completely worn out in every sense of the word, but it's a gesture that brings tears to my eyes. Kaida's thoughtfulness will forever be a breath of fresh air to me and a balm to my soul.

As I read, the toll of the day weighs on my eyelids, causing them to droop more until I doze off before reaching chapter two. Peacefully, I nap in my chair, the quiet evening acting as a blanket for my senses. I don't move again until the next day, the morning's rays of light are slipping through the cracks of the curtains, the sun waking me with a smile.

Apology Accepted

It's been two days since our success at the market, and I'm sitting in the study, making my plan for next week, when someone raps at the door, loudly. I wait, ignoring the noise instead of rising, not wanting to stop what I'm doing. The knocking continues, and since I don't hear Kaida, I rise from my seat with a protesting groan.

I glance out the window as I shuffle to the door, only to be struck by a wave of surprise. For whatever reason, Jareth is on the other side of the door, rocking on the heels of his shoes with his hands in his pockets.

Slowly, I open the door. "May I help you?" The crisp air blows past me, traveling further into the house. A second gust sends a shiver down my body.

Maybe it's the way I hold the door, similar to the way he did the day we met, or maybe it's the wary expression on my face. Either way, he seems nervous. Hoping to prompt him into speaking, I raise a brow and tilt my head. This seems to remind him of his reason for visiting, because he speaks, though it's slow and almost too quiet at first.

"Oh, erm, yes. I, uh, wanted to.. You know. Apologize. For the way I spoke to you and Kaida that day you came to my house. It was incredibly rude, and I- I wanted to let you know that I am incredibly sorry." His eyes dart from me to the ground, not moving as he fumbles through his awkward apology. "I just.. I'm not good with others socially. According to Ms. Kestrel, I lack social skills, especially when I get nervous around new people. I forget that not every thought shouldn't be spoken, and I'm worried that I may have offended the two of you by not considering my words before speaking them."

I stand in front of him, still as a statue. I don't know what I had expected him to say, but this definitely isn't it. I don't even know how to respond to him. Thankfully, Kaida saves me from embarrassing myself by bouncing to the door, yanking it open wider, and smiling brightly at him. "Apology accepted, Sir Cranky! Now get in here before you let all the warm air out. It's a bit chilly out there today. Besides, I just finished baking the most incredible cinnamon chocolate chip bread for dessert tonight, and I'm currently finishing up some bread bowls for the soup Eilaen is making." Kaida says, moving to let Jareth into the house.

Once the door is closed, she rambles, her words pouring out of her rapidly. "Bet ya didn't know that it's Eilaen who cooks while I bake. Most people think that just because I can bake, I can cook, but that's not true. I try, but nothing I cook turns out edible, so Eilaen cooks, and I bake. It's our agreement, and it's the only reason dinner isn't burnt every night. You would not want me to cook. Phew! No, sir, you would not. We'd be eating charred vegetables and burnt meat. It would be a disaster! This way."

Jareth and I follow her into the kitchen, his face lighting in awe as he watches the bread bowls rise into the air and fly towards us when she opens the oven with a flick of her wrist. The smell of buttery garlic and fresh bread fills the air and has my mouth watering even before the bowls make their way onto the island, my stomach grumbling its complaint to be empty even with Kaida's baking in front of me.

Jareth's face transforms from awe to astonishment as his eyes dart from Kaida to the bread, and then back to my best friend, who stands on the island with her hands on her hips as she wears a proud smile. I yank on the sleeve of Jareth's shirt, pulling him to the stools on the opposite side of her before leaning over to snatch a discarded hunk of the warm bread that Kaida discards while cutting the rounded loaves into bowls.

With a happy sigh and a little wiggle of a dance, I walk to

the pantry and grab the ingredients I'll need for the vegetable stew that I'm cooking for supper tonight. I can practically taste the way the soup and bread mingle together in my mouth, prompting me to move quicker. With everything in hand, I turn towards the stove and toss some butter into the large stock pot waiting for me. With precision, I dice an onion and a stick of celery before peeling and dicing the carrots.

I let the vegetables cook, sauteeing them until the onions are almost caramelized before removing them from the heat. To my left, I sear beef stew chunks in two large heaps of butter. The scents of everything cooking mix together, the aroma causing all three of our stomachs to grumble loudly. Finally, I add the beef to the other ingredients, which have been waiting in the stock pot, and finish by adding a variety of vegetables and a large jar of beef stock.

All that's left to do is wait.

I clap my hands together and turn to Kaida and Jareth. "Well, I've finished my part. Now it's time for the soup and the heat to do theirs. Let's go into the den while we wait. It'll help to keep the food from tormenting us."

Nodding in agreement, they follow me, and we sit in the chairs, an awkward silence stretching out over us.

Maybe we should get to know our guest, I think to myself, but before I can say his name, Kaida whips her head towards me, her eyes wide.

"Please tell me you remembered to invite Ms. Kestrel over for dinner tonight, Eilean," she frantically asks.

I look at her, trying to keep a neutral expression. "Yes, Kai, I did. Don't worry. She said she'd be here before the sun was fully set."

Kaida sighs in relief and looks at Jareth, who is looking between Kaida and me, confused. "I hope you don't mind, but we had already had plans with Ms. Kestrel for dinner tonight. I hate the idea of her dining alone so much, so we try to get her over here at least twice a week."

"I don't mind one bit," he says, shrugging his shoulders nonchalantly. "In fact, I don't know a single soul who doesn't care for her. Ms. Kestrel is probably the only reason I haven't been forced out of Smallburrow, ya know, on account of my lack of social ability. I don't think I would have had anyone to talk to had she not continued to visit me after Mrs. Mapleground passed."

His voice holds a hint of sadness to it, and for the first time, I consider the possibility that Jareth's stand-offish demeanor might be a result of how close he was to my grandparents before their deaths.

The truth swirls within me that he knew them better than I ever have, a thought that tastes bittersweet. I was never given the chance to get to know my grandparents, whereas Jareth was their neighbor long enough that their deaths still grieve him, even if just slightly.

For the first time since meeting him, I want to reach out and grab his hand, ask questions, and try to learn whatever I can about them, even if it's through his eyes. My thirst for knowledge and answers mixes with genuine curiosity, and there's a little voice in the back of my mind pushing me to seek the information I desire, no matter the cost. The rational part of me knows that pushing too soon or too hard might not end the way I want, though.

Either way, my mind fills with a hundred questions instantly, and I have to bite my tongue to stop from word vomiting all of them at his feet. After debating on which question to ask first, I decide the best one to start with is the simplest. "What did you do for my grandparents, Jareth?"

It's such a simple question that I'm puzzled when his mouth parts and his eyes widen in surprise. He lets a few moments go by, his hands tapping his legs steadily before answering, as if he's debating on where to start, which builds the impatient anticipation in me.

"When I moved here, I was down on my luck and desperate for work. More than that, though, I was desperate for a sense of family with people who respected me. Your grandparents, gods bless them, gave me all of that and so much more. I assisted Mr. Mapleground with the farm by tending and harvesting the plants while also helping Mrs. Mapleground with heavy lifting and anything around the house she needed. Even though they paid me for my help, they still treated me like I'd been born into the family. Or, rather, your family. It was as if I was as close as they'd get to the son they'd been missing." His eyes shine, and his mouth turns down as unshed tears build on his lash lines. His thumbs twiddle around one another as he sits silent.

I wonder what memories are running through his mind now. Should I ask? Will that make it weird? I nod slowly, wishing for the hundredth time I could find the line between what's socially acceptable and what's too intrusive.

"Where's your family from, Jareth?" Kaida asks tenderly after giving him the chance to collect himself.

"They're in Elvenden. I knew from an early age that I wanted to live somewhere on my own, somewhere that lives life at a much slower pace than that of the busy elves and Fae. The hustle and bustle has always been too much for me to manage. I like my surroundings a little chaotic, but I also like them when I can choose the amount of chaos I participate in, and that's not something I was in control of back home. In the end, I decided to leave on my own." He stares at his hands again and sighs.

"Without their blessing, I made the long journey out here to start fresh. Sometimes, my mother will send a card or letter, and I may see them once or twice a year. But that's pretty much the extent of our contact. News of me moving wasn't received well, and my father still holds it against me," Jareth trails off with a shrug that isn't as careless as he tries to play it off as. Or that's what I assume when he refuses to meet our eyes again.

Before either Kaida or I can give him any empathetic words, a knock sounds from the door, and Ms. Kestrel's voice is heard in the den after the second knock. She wanders into the room with a shiny contraption that looks like it would make a great object to open doors, swinging from her wrist. "Evenin' girlies! It's a bit chilly out there this evening. Hello, Jareth boy. I see you've finally decided to stop being a ninny and make your way over to the girls' table." With a sigh, the elderly gnome drapes her cloak on the back of the sofa and tucks her new gadget into the inside pocket of it. After shuffling to the other side of the room, she plops onto the sofa's cushion with a weary sound.

"Hello, Ms. Kestrel. It's lovely to see you, as always,"

Jareth says, standing before taking two steps and embracing her tightly.

An unusual sensation of warmth and emotion runs through me, with watering eyes, I excuse myself to the kitchen, where the mouth-watering scent of tonight's dinner slams into me. After giving the stew a good taste test, I cry out to Kaida for help, and she quickly appears, grabbing the dishes. I wait until the plates are in front of me before pouring stew into the bread bowls, my stomach growling loudly as the smell gets stronger and more appetizing. Together, we step into the dining room, a plate in each hand, and set them on the large, dark table, and then return to the kitchen for the cutlery and drinks. Once everything is in its place, we call our guests into the dining room for our meal.

As the evening progresses, we all sit around while laughing and eating to our hearts' content. After everyone has gotten their fill of stew, Kaida and I collect everyone's plates and return with the cake she has spent most of her day working on. We all gush over her skills, Jareth and Ms. Kestrel gasping in awe at how incredible it looks. The chocolate cake has chocolate icing and is topped with handmade edible flowers. Though I'm accustomed to seeing the amazing things my friend can concoct, it never fails to fill me with pride for her whenever someone compliments her on her abilities.

Between mouthfuls of cake, Jareth raves about the dessert. "This. Is. The. Best. Cake. I have. Ever. Eaten," he sputters, cake crumbs flying from his mouth as he emphasises each word.

Kaida blushes at his compliment, and her smile stretches wider when Ms. Kestrel agrees with him. "He's right, girlie. This is the best treat you've served me yet. Everything tonight has been nothing less than splendid. You should both be very proud of yourselves."

She gives us both the warm, grandmotherly smile that we've already come to associate with her before stabbing her fork into her cake once more.

"Thank you both very much!" Kaida replies, her hands clapping together excitedly. "Cakes are one of my absolute favorite things to create. There is just so much that you can do with them."

Knowing what always comes next when Kaida's on the topic of cakes, I try to interrupt and beg her not to, but she keeps speaking and launches into an incredibly detailed ramble about cake textures, flavors, types of frosting, and garnishments. It's a topic that I frequently find myself in the middle of, having heard it enough to recite her spiel word for word, even down to the hand gestures. One would think Kaida would have changed it over the years, but she hasn't, and I roll my eyes with a smile as I listen to her talk about her love of cakes and baking.

Being friends with Kaida is like that. Her passion is so great that I'm convinced she could make anyone fall in love with the idea of baking, even if they're like me and have never been successful at anything considered a baked good.

By the time her almost-speech is done, everyone's tea is cold, and our bellies are fuller than full. The sky outside is slipping further and further into the navy shade of night by the second. When they see how dark it is outside, both Jareth and Ms. Kestrels rise in preparation for heading home.

Before leaving, Jareth hugs both of us as if we were old friends. It's weird and makes me slightly uncomfortable, and I'm so focused on keeping my face from speaking that I can't keep my muscles from stiffening. Thankfully, he doesn't seem to notice.

"Thank you for inviting me over for supper tonight. It was nice, and I enjoyed the company more than you'll ever know. I look forward to our next meal together. Eilaen, I'll bring those books that we discussed over soon." He quickly makes it to the door, his long stride twice the length of my own, and waves at us before leaving.

With a large yawn, Ms. Kestrel jumps down to the floor, her short legs kicking back and forth as she slides off the couch. "Yet another wonderful meal, girlies. Thank ya for once again inviting me over to dinner. Your kindness in allowing an old gnome like me into your home and around your table is a blessing to be sure. As the old Gnomish proverb says, 'may the ground always prove to be fruitful for you as long as you shall live'."

She shuffles around the sofa and pulls her cloak off its

back and tosses it around her shoulders, moving her hand to her pocket to pull the contraction from earlier out of it. With my head leaning to the side in wonder, I watch as she raises it and latches it onto the doorknob. Wonder shifts to amazement when she squeezes a trigger, and the device allows her to twist the knob with ease. Before closing the door, I watch as she repeats the process once she's on the front step.

I give her enough time to reach the gate before locking the door. Once it's locked, I check and then double-check if the door is actually locked. After the third check, my brain is finally convinced that I won't come down tomorrow to find the door wide open like when I came down to find Tillard snoring on the sofa one morning last week.

The pink, hairy pig had given me such a fright that my scream woke him, which then had him running around squealing. It took me too long to get his muddy self out of the farmhouse and back into the pen where he belongs. Truly an experience that I never wish to experience again as long as I live. I genuinely believe that when I die, it'll be because of that meathead and his shenanigans.

I'm still shaking my head at the memory when I meet Kaida in the kitchen so we can clean up from our meal and tuck in our kitchen for the night. The unfamiliar sensation stirring in me hits me as I enter my room, still puzzling me when I slide under the blanket. I look at the ceiling for a while, trying to sort through it and discover what it means, though I remain unsuccessful. Finally, I close my eyes and give in to the sleep that wishes to pull me under, giving in at last.

The Magic of Friendship

Morning arrives too quickly and, when I wake, the first thing I notice is that it's cold everywhere that's not under my blanket. No, cold doesn't even describe it accurately. It's freezing. So much so that I can see my breath as I exhale.

This is so strange. Why is it so cold in here? It's too early in the year for such a drastic temperature shift to occur overnight. When my feet touch the floor, I wince from the sting caused by the icy wooden planks. I quickly find my slippers to prevent stepping on the floor more than possible and then wrap my thicker housecoat around me, tying it as tightly as I can. I descend the stairs, vigorously rubbing my hands up and down my arms. I reach the last step and hear Kaida complaining, finding her trying to strike a fire unsuccessfully.

"Why's it so cold, Kai?" I ask, now rubbing my hands together to warm my frozen digits. My teeth are chattering so hard, I'm scared I'll break a tooth or bite my tongue off.

It's too early for this.

Teeth clacking together, Kaida's normally cheery face looks at me, her expression pinched and grumpy. "I do-don't kn-kn-know, Ellie. But when I w-woke up, it was so cold that I thought my bum would turn into an ice block on the t-t-toilet and I could see my breath when I breathed." Kaida gives up on the fire, stuffing her hands into her pockets, and turns in the direction of the kitchen. "I'm going to light the wood stove and toss on a kettle for some warmth. It's so cold that my fingers won't be any use for baking." With a huff, she leaves me at the fireplace alone.

When I finally get a match to light, the flicker morphs into a wave of flames and I huddle next to the blaze, wiggling my extremities in hopes they'll be quicker to thaw. As the fire grows, the head spreads out further and the heat seeps into my body deliciously, defrosting me within moments.

The faint sound of an unhappy rooster startles me, reminding me that the animals are in similar conditions and also need something to keep them from the harmful effects the weather can cause. I run up the stairs as quickly as I can and throw clothing on, shoving my feet into my boots as I run out the door so I can take care of them.

I slide down the pathway, coming to a sudden stop before reaching the end. Grief bubbles in my gut at the sight in front of me and my heart shatters. To my dismay, the entire garden, which had been green and thriving just yesterday, has died overnight. There is now frost coating the surface of every single plant in front of me.

I'll deal with this after I tend the animals, I tell myself, forcing my feet to move so I can race across the field and to the barn. The trough has a thick layer of ice over its surface, and I have no idea how to fix that. As I walk into the barn, I remember that there is a small wooden stove in the furthest corner and I'm fairly certain it's for circumstances such as these. I stuff small wooden chunks into it and light it, sighing in relief whenever the fire catches in a fraction of the time that it did inside the house. The heat doesn't take long to take the chill out of the air and by the time I'm done tending the cows and pigs, the barn is comfortable instead of being igloo-like.

Once I see that the animals have relaxed, I move to the stable and locate an identical wooden stove. Like the one in the barn, this one lights almost instantly which allows me to care for Sorrel and Mabel quickly. I have similar success in the chicken coop and once I know that all of the animals are warm and cozy, I take off towards the garden to determine the extent of the damage.

I already know it's going to be decimated, I can sense it deep down somehow. There's a pull to do something, anything, to save it which does nothing but leave me feeling overwhelmed as a sense of failure spreads through me at my inability to change it. The more I look, the more my heart breaks. Every tree, every fruit, every vegetable, every herb... There's nothing to salvage here.

A sob catches in my throat as the tears building in my eyes cause my vision to grow blurry. As they trail down my cheeks, I drop my head in defeat and walk to the house. I should just give up. *This is a sign that I never should have gone through with this move or made such a large change. How incredibly stupid was I to think I could do this?* A cruel laugh escapes with this thought as I continue to berate myself. *I was delusional. There is no way this was going to work. Of course, my dream is over before it actually had a chance to begin.*

As I reach for the doorknob, a voice cries out my name and I spin around to see Jareth sprinting through the gate and towards me. I meet him halfway, my face twisted in confusion.

Gasping, he stops running and bends over, placing his hands on his knees. "Eilaen... The garden.. How.. Bad?" It's hard to understand him clearly between the wheezing and coughing that wrack through him as he attempts to catch his breath, and I assume it's from the bite in the air.

It takes a moment to process his question as I wonder why he's even here, standing as if tongue-tied until it dawns on me that he probably has a magic that can help. "I'm pretty sure everything is dead. And if it isn't dead, then it's almost there." The admission has the tears building again.

"Follow me," Jareth says, striding towards the garden, not bothering to look back to see if I'm following him or not. When I finally catch up to him, which takes a moment between how short my legs are and the cold, he is surveying the icy mess the garden has become. "When Mr. Mapleground was alive, he'd have me come assist him during these random ice spells, too. They don't happen too often, thank goodness. But when they do, I'm sure it's nice to have a Fae with a proclivity for nature magic living next door when they do."

Cautiously, I watch as he closes his eyes and hovers his hand—palm down—over the plot directly in front of him, my body poised to run away should a disaster occur. As a soft yellow light surges from his palm, my eyes open widely and my mouth opens as I watch the light grow brighter. For a moment, I wonder if anything else is going to happen, but before I can ask, the plants in the first row transform, their stalks a healthy shade of green.

I refuse to blink, not wanting to miss anything and by the time my eyes dry out from the frigid air, everything in the plot at my feet is alive once again. I blink rapidly, pinching my arm to ensure I'm really awake.

"I... You... That was just... Wait, what?" I ask, stammering as I follow behind. I watch, pinching myself several more times, as we travel through the garden as Jareth repeats the process every few steps. He doesn't stop moving until every fruit, vegetable, and herb is as bright and healthy as when I went to bed last night.

As creepy as it might be, I cannot stop staring at him. Nobody I know, other than Kaida, has used magic in front of me as if using it is just as natural as breathing. A chill runs down my spine, and I can't be certain if it's from the weather or from what I just witnessed.

Either way, it takes a few moments but eventually, my ability to speak finally reappears. "W-would you like to come in for tea and breakfast? Kaida was starting some pastries when I bolted out here this morning, and I know she'd be rather irritated if I didn't at least ask you in," I ask with, what I hope is a small smile. It's hard to know for certain with how cold my face is and the lack of feeling I currently possess in my cheeks.

"Oh, yeah. Absolutely. That would be fantastic," he replies without hesitation.

Frozen, the two of us walk awkwardly towards the house, the sun finally making its appearance, its rays warming my face just as I move to open the door. Taking a step forward, we both attempt to step through the doorway at the same time, realizing immediately that it'll be impossible to do so.

I take a step back and motion for him to step inside before me, my mind a jumbled mess as I go through the motions to wipe off my feet on the doormat before remembering I need to take my boots off first. After I direct him to the den and encourage him to sit and warm up, I head into the kitchen, all the while trying to remind myself that what I witnessed is the same thing as watching Kaida use her magic. Unfortunately for me, my brain refuses to accept that and it's almost impossible for me to recognize his ability as a part of him rather than an incredible work done by him.

Logically, I know that the only difference in baking magic and whatever it is that Jareth possesses is the type it is. So why is it so hard for me to move past the tugging I felt when he used it in front of me?

After warring with myself, I finally settle on the answer being that this is nothing like what I see in Kaida whenever she uses hers. His magic is much different, much more than what Kaida possesses. Something about it makes me far too uneasy, but why that is remains unclear.

Suddenly, my mind recalls something he said the day we met when he mentioned letting him know if the garden failed and we needed assistance. At the time, I thought he meant that he'd lend a hand should we need help. But what if this is what he meant? What if that wasn't for the eventual pickle we'd find ourselves in, but rather when the need for the plants to be restored became emergent?

The realization clicks in my mind, solidifying his meaning. What he'd said hadn't come out correctly, which makes more sense now that I know he'd been rude without meaning to that day. He was trying to be helpful through his grief and lack of social skills, letting us know that he genuinely would assist should we need it, like this morning. With his nature magic.

"Kai, we've gotta talk. Now. Is there any water left in the kettle?" I call out as I enter the kitchen.

"Yeh. But can you help me with something right quick? I'm quite literally elbow deep in this dough." Kaida loudly responds and I'm met with her laughing at whatever she's gotten herself into.

I move to the island where she stands, dough literally up to her elbows, unable to tell if my heart is pounding because she needs my assistance or if it's from what I'm about to tell her.

Quickly, I look over my shoulder to see if Jareth stayed in the den and then lean into her space.

"What's wrong with you?" Kaida asks, trying to lean away from me.

"Kaida, you will never believe who is in our den right at this moment," I whisper, though my volume is much louder than it should be in my slightly panicked state.

"Is it the mayor?" Kaida asks playfully before taking note of my tone. "Wait. What's going on? Why are we whispering?" Her whisper isn't even a whisper, her giggle disrupting from her mock serious expression.

I groan at her frustratedly. "No, you nut. Not the mayor. Jareth. You know, Jareth? The Fae next door? He's in our den, sitting on our couch and warming up under our blankets. And do you know why he's in there? Because he just saved every bit of our garden with his hands. His hands, Kaida Louise." I rasp frantically.

She stops moving, peering at me through narrow eyes with her head cocked to the side. "Whatdya mean by his hands? Did you get kicked by a cow again, Ellie? Honestly, maybe you shouldn't be allowed to milk the cows by yourself anymore."

"You know, Kai, you can be a rightly rude ninny sometimes. Keep on and you'll stay elbow deep in that dough while I waltz back into the den and snuggle under a blanket by the fire." I reply plainly, planting my hands on my hips and sticking my tongue out at her.

"Ohhhhh-kay. Okay. Start at the beginning and explain this whole thing to me. Whatever it is. What happened out there? Oh, and while you're explaining it, I need you to get me three eggs, a big bowl, and some of those mashed cinnamon apples from the muffins I made yesterday morning." Kaida turns her eyes back to the dough, which seems to have grown exponentially in the time we've been standing here, trying to conceal how amused she is at my exasperation.

In my haste to explain everything to her, I forgot to listen for the sounds of Jareth's steps, and because of this, our neighbor appears next to me in the kitchen, startling the breath out of me.

"Well, it's hard for her to explain something that she

hasn't personally experienced. We all know that most halflings can't produce magic spontaneously without having a magical being in their lineage at some point. As magical as their cooking skills are, it's not quite the same." Jareth interrupts, leaning against the clean side of the island.

"It's actually fairly simple. The Fae in my family have always had a pretty intense affinity for nature magic, especially when it comes to gardening. We have the ability to heal plants or harm them, depending on our moods and intentions. When Mr. Mapleground found out what I could do, he asked if I could help keep the garden from dying between spring and autumn so that he could make sure the town stayed fed. I'm sure you've noticed just how quickly your produce sells on market days. That's because your farm is one of the few in our area. Of those few, it's the largest and has the widest variety of crops. So, it only makes sense to everyone that we keep it well-tended and alive for as long as possible for the town's benefit." He shrugs, picking up his cup of tea and sipping at it.

"Oh. So that's why you said to come get you if we had any trouble?" Kaida's eyes get wide. "Wait, wait. I have questions for you and I desperately need your answers. Start with the basics. How does it work? How fast do your stores empty? What are your limitations?" Kaida asks, her questions firing rapidly.

Instead of being annoyed, he laughs at her interrogation. "This tea is warm and all, and I am definitely up to answer all questions, but would it be too much to ask for something to eat before we dive into it? I have a feeling you have more questions than that, and after all the work I put in this morning, I'm starving." He takes a bite of the day-old cinnamon apple muffin I hand him, groaning at its deliciousness before continuing. "To grow the plants, I have to keep my emotions and intentions positive. That keeps me from accidentally killing them. Then, I place my hands over the plants with my palms facing the ground and put all of my focus on what I need to do, whether that be healing the plants like this morning, or growing them should they need to grow quicker than usual. When my hands glow and warm up, the magic kicks in and everything is right as it should be."

"And your negative emotions then? They do the opposite?"

I ask, amazed at what he's telling us.

"Exactly," he replies, pointing a finger at me with one hand as the other crams the remainder of his muffin into his mouth.

When the conversation doesn't progress, I look over and ask, "How much longer until those pastries are done, Kai?"

"Not too much longer. Actually, I'd say right about... Now!" she replies with a dance, smiling as she waves her fingers in an upward motion. In response, the wood stove opens and a thin pan slides out of it that she, then, motions towards the towel on the counter beside it.

In an instant, the air fills with the scents of burning wood, chocolate, and strawberry from the miniature chocolate-covered strawberry pies Kaida whipped up on a whim while I was outside with the animals and garden.

"These smell delicious," Jareth groans when Kaida hands one to him, and together, we each grab our tea and treats and move into the den.

When I sense someone staring at me, I look up and notice that Jareth is looking at me with a puzzled look on his face. Not wanting to draw any additional attention to myself, I ignore him while also making a mental note to ask Kaida if she had noticed any reason for his staring or if he's just weird.

We sit comfortably, finishing our food in peace. Once he's emptied his teacup, he stands and thanks us for the warm breakfast. He stands at the door for a moment, opening it and then closing it immediately before walking back into the den.

"I know I've said it and you have already accepted my apology, but I wanted to say I'm sorry, again. I really shouldn't have been so hateful when you came to my door. I hope we can move forward as friends." His hand covers the back of his neck and he rubs the skin nervously. "Oh, and Kaida? Can you make me some more of those raspberry tartlets? I'd like to purchase a dozen for pickup at the market, please."

Kaida agrees and when he opens the door this time, he closes it after he walks through it. I watch out of the window, perplexed, as he walks down the path, through the gate, and toward his house, still uncertain of what to make of him.

"What an odd day this has turned out to be," I murmur to

myself as I settle into my chair and pick up the book next to me. As I flip to the page I stopped on, I realize that my morning routine has yet to be anything close to normal, yet I haven't spun out of control mentally or emotionally. Pride blossoms through me at this, especially when I take in how destructive this would have been before now.

When my routine had been disturbed in the past, whether simply disturbed or missed completely, I would fall apart completely. Nobody knows why, not even myself. Hazy memories of the time my parents took me to the physician still linger. I was only four or five, but I remember us storming out of the clinic moments after the physician had used words like "high strung" and "anxiety riddled" and "obsessive compulsion" or something of the sort.

To this day, I'm still unsure why I'm compelled to do the things I do. All I know is that when I don't, my day may as well be ruined and my emotions spin wildly out of control. But today? Today has felt as if I've been given a little extra freedom, the weight of the irrational impending doom nowhere to be found.

This adventure is definitely proving to be utterly life-changing in more ways than I could have ever thought possible.

Market Day Mischief

As more mornings bring in the frost that covers the plants, the wooden stoves in the stable, barn, and coop are putting in just as much work as I am by chopping the wood and hauling it into each building to ensure they'd stay warm at night. On the plus side, Jareth living next door means I have someone available to assist in the heavier parts of the task, like moving the logs to the chopping stump. Subtly, however, we soon notice that Jareth's visits get closer together until there's not more than a day or two that passes without him showing up at least once a day.

If I'm being honest, having Jareth around constantly isn't necessarily the worst thing I've had to endure in my lifetime, but it's a lot like having a brother that I never asked for who loves to pick at me until he grates my nerves; or so I've been told anyway. I wouldn't know as an only child. It's not that he is necessarily what irks me, but rather the way he's always there when I'm rounding the corner of the house in the mornings. Or maybe it's the fact that he seems to honestly believe he belongs at our house every waking moment of the day more often than not.

I squint at him and picture his face on a mushroom or a fungus-like growth, like one of those kinds that appear overnight and take over everything in sight. To make things even worse? He's a morning person, one of those who has a bright and cheery kind of guys who carries this disposition with him wherever he goes. You know who isn't a morning person? Neither Kaida nor I, and this is why our system works so well.

Kaida's day starts with her waking up alone and preparing

for her daily baking, while I, on the other hand, love tending to the animals and garden tasks without anyone trying to talk to me. As long as Tillard behaves, there's nobody I have to talk to until I'm ready. By the time we tell each other good morning, Kaida and I are already awake and starting our days, and are more than ready to chit-chat as we eat second breakfast, making us happier to be around as a whole.

I'm roughly halfway through feeding the animals when it occurs to me that Jareth hasn't been by in around three to four days, and blast it if that doesn't drag up a pea-sized worry spot in my gut. As I continue to go about my business, he periodically pops into my mind.

I hope he's okay. Maybe we should check on him...

Annoyed, I grumble as I stomp through the field towards the garden. "Not even here, and that pesky Fae still manages to annoy me."

Lost in my own world, I'm jarringly pulled back into reality when Kaida yanks my arm as I head into the house and yells, "Come on, Ellie! We're going to be late if we don't get a move on!"

I open my mouth to protest until I see the wicker baskets swinging around her elbows. Oh no! I cannot believe I forgot we have to be at the market this morning, even though we had compiled our wares before bed last night. "I cannot believe this," I whisper under my breath as I shove potatoes, carrots, and corncobs into baskets before running the produce outside.

When I run into the house again to grab the cheese I made last week and the eggs I collected this moment, I see the fresh milk still sitting on the counter, and I slap my forehead.

How can I be so forgetful?

Any lingering thought I may have had for Jareth or his well-being no longer exists as I hurry through hitching Mabel to the wagon and jump into the seat next to Kaida, who wasted no time before spurring the horse into action. My heart thrums inside my chest, beating erratically enough for me to wonder if it can actually beat straight through me.

We ride down the road as quickly as Mabel can physically carry us. After a moment, she hands me a muffin as a reminder to eat.

"Oh, don't forget that you also have a cup of lavender and honey tea in the basket waiting for you when we get unloaded and settled in. I knew buying those stones would come in handy!" The satisfied grin she wears practically screams "I told you so," even though she doesn't say it.

"Fine," I relent between bites. "You were right, and I was wrong. But honestly, Kai. How was I supposed to know how soon the enchanted warming stones you stumbled on last week would come in handy? That wasn't even one of the Market's merchants. It was a traveling merchant passing through!"

"That is true," she muses. Still, the grin stays in place. "You do have to admit that they're going to make market days more enjoyable, especially since there are more chilly days than there aren't right now."

I hum in agreement, finishing my food as we pass into town, and we can see customers lining up in front of Number One Booth waiting patiently for us to arrive and open. We've barely come to a stop when we're met by several market assistants who offer to carry some of our wares to our table.

Ms. Kestrel is first in line and moseys up to us with a warm expression on her face. "You were almost late, girlies." She arches her brow and chuckles. "But you're here now, and that's all that matters. Kaida, I would like to place an order for a loaf of sweet bread and two orders of cookies. Eilaen, can I get one of those slabs of garlic and herb-infused butter, as well as a dozen eggs?"

We bundle her order and hand it to her as she slides the coins across the table. Bidding us a good day and promising to come to the house soon, she shuffles away so the line can move forward. From that moment, it's impossible to take a moment to breathe, our booth busier than it's been thus far. The loud sounds and voices overlapping from so many people talking pierce through my ears and go straight into my brain; the resulting thundering noise that occurs when I blink is almost too much for me to stomach. A wave of nausea rolls through me, causing my breakfast to threaten to revolt.

Finally, we hit a lull that can almost be described as magical, and we're able to sit down and take a break. Kaida unpacks the small basket she'd prepared for us that includes two sandwiches, a couple of pastries each, and the thick glass jar that holds our tea. The warmth that radiates from it being on top of the stones thaws my fingers, relieving the ache that has been forming for the last hour or so.

I practically inhale my food, throwing myself back with a huff and thanking the stars that there's less foot traffic right now than before our break. I can almost consider my surroundings to be peaceful. Then I hear it.

That laugh. Too late do I realize how loud my groan is, and Kaida turns to me with a mischievous glint in her eye and a perfect green brow raised.

"What's the matter, Ellie?" Kaida asks, but I can see by the expression on her face that she already knows what's prompted my distress.

"I think you already know the answer to that, Kaida," I grumble, scrunching my face in annoyance. Three booths down stands Jareth, laughing with several of the townsfolk as he waves his hands animatedly.

"So? We see him all the time. What's the big deal?" Kaida shrugs. "Besides, what's wrong with him? You always seem so put off by his presence, and I know it's not because he's ugly. He's actually not too bad to stare at, being cute in that Fae kind of way and all."

I collect my thoughts before speaking, not wanting to trip over my words. Why am I so bothered right now when I was concerned about him earlier? I don't know, but I know I need to answer Kaida's question before she creates an assumption and sticks to it—if she hasn't already done so.

I roll my eyes as she leans closer to me, hinting that she's ready for whatever I'm going to say. "Well, let's see. He's loud, for one. And he talks a lot first thing in the morning. I mean, come on. Who does that? And not only that, but he's constantly in my space, and I do mean constantly. There's never a reason to get that close to someone. Ever." My face gets hot, and I'm sure it's now the same shade of red as the tomato sitting to my left.

"And then there's his magic. It just... He just makes me feel strange." I look down, not wanting to see whatever goofy face it is that I know she's making, but look up when I realize she's waiting to speak until she knows I'm paying attention; this always means I have to fake looking her in the eye and train my sight on her nose or forehead since eye contact makes me feel more than uncomfortable.

She makes a triumphant noise before cocking her head to the side. Her twinkling eyes squint as they dart back and forth across my face as if she's trying to find something written on it. I wrinkle my forehead and lean away. "What are you doing, Kaida Louise?"

Instead of leaning back, she only gets further, not stopping until her nose is practically smooshed against mine. "What do you mean, strange? Like in a magicky kind of way?" She bolts upright, and her eyes widen. "Wait, wait. Ellie, tell me. Is it in a magicky kind of way? Or is it a romancey kind of way?" With her lips puckered, she makes the most obnoxious kissing noises in the air.

"Kaida," I hiss. My face twists in disgust at the accusation."Stop it right now, you nut. You're... Would you stop that before you make a scene? I know exactly what you are implying, and I don't think I've heard you spout such incorrect nonsense in all the years I've known you. So to answer your question, no, I do not have a silly girl's crush on Jareth. How preposterous," I whisper loudly. "And if you must know, no. It's definitely not in a romancey kind of way. But how am I supposed to know if it's because of magic? I can't do magic. All I know is that, whatever it is, it tugs at me only when we're working together in the garden. At first, I thought I was just reacting to his magic as he healed the plants, then I assumed it was all in my head. But it only happens whenever we're tending to the plants in the garden. Never inside, never here."

"Wow, Ellie. You almost sound as if you really mean it when you say I'm speaking nonsense."

"That's because I do mean it, Kaida Louise," I say. I take a deep breath, trying to squash the exasperation this conversation has caused.

"Okay, I'll drop it then," she replies, patting my arm.

"Thank you," I say, turning away to restock the table.

Then, as if hearing us talk about him, Jareth appears directly in front of me, his face happy and bright. "Good afternoon, neighbors. How are we today?" Without waiting for either of us to answer, he continues speaking.

"Sorry that I haven't been by in a few days. I've been busy helping Mayor Luddie and Council-orc Urzal plan and organize the Autumn Festival. We're planning on really making a big event this year, so it's taken more meetings for us to get ourselves together before we get the townsfolk involved."

"Did I hear what I think I heard? An Autumn Festival?" Kaida squeals, her excitement obvious to anyone within a four-booth radius. "I haven't heard of that! Tell me more! I wanna hear all about it." From our side of the booth, she clutches his arm and shakes him.

Jareth laughs and peels her fingers off of him. "The Autumn Festival is the one day during autumn that we celebrate the founding of Smallburrow. There are games, a maze, several contests, and a handful of traveling merchants and booths where some of the townsfolk sell the wares that can only be found during the festival. Before the maze, we celebrate with a feast that everyone contributes to."

"When is it?" I ask.

"The day before winter begins, which means we only have two weeks to get things going. There's a lot we've gotta do, and not that much time to do it in."

Kaida's eyes widen, and another squeal erupts from her. "That sounds like so much fun! I love this town so much. Speaking of celebrations, did you know Eilaen's birthday is coming up?" I kick her underneath the table, but she doesn't take the hint. "Actually, it's in two days!"

My ears burn from having so much attention on me between the two of them, and all I want to do is curl into myself until I'm so small that nobody can see me. "Oh, hush, Kai. Nobody cares for my birthday but you," I finally manage to say, waving my hand in her direction.

Kaida opens her mouth as if to protest, but before she can, Jareth says, "I wouldn't say nobody, Eilaen. Thank you, Kaida, for being neighborly and saving me the footwork of finding this information. I'll have to jot it down on the birthday list Urzal keeps for the merchants." He rubs his hands together, the loud noise from the friction grating on my senses. "Now, for more important things. Please tell me you saved me some cinnamon apple pastries. I've been dying for one all morning!"

As Kaida reaches under the table to grab the package of pastries she specifically packed up for him, she laughs and teases him by holding his prize out of reach until he slides the coins towards her. Package in hand, he thanks her and bows to the two of us, waving as he walks away.

My hands cover my face as I breathe slowly, thankful for him leaving and the relief it has brought me. When I uncover my face, Kaida's cheery face is staring at me, and she grins mischievously. "Ya know, Ellie. You really could do much worse than a good lookin' Fae male who helps in the garden, loves my baking, and looks at you as if you happen to be his best friend in the whole wide world."

She doesn't give me a chance to respond before she slides off her chair, grabs the empty baskets at her feet, and carries them to the wagon as quickly as her stocky legs will carry her.

Happy Birthday, Eilaen Mapleground!

The morning of my birthday, I wake and attend business as usual, no recollection whatsoever of the conversation between Jareth, Kaida, and me or any remembrance of today's date. It's not until I finish my chores and walk into the house, the door closing behind me as I slip my boots off, that I smell my favorite scent in the world: Kaida's homemade pumpkin cake. The mouth-watering aroma pulls me in, summoning me towards the kitchen where I hear hushed tones of Kaida whispering to, I assume, herself.

Happy birthday to me, happy birthday to me. It's pumpkin cake day, Eilaen. Happy birthday to me.

I giggle at the song in my mind, humming it as I step through the dining room. What I find in the kitchen, however, is not what I was expecting, which is Kaida being elbow deep in whatever dough she has been preparing since sunrise. Instead, I see her smiling widely with our neighbors, the three of them standing apparently waiting on something.

Are they waiting for me? I'm so surprised that I can't speak or move, and I'm wholly unsure what I should be doing with my hands. Or my eyes. Am I even breathing right now?

"Happy birthday!" they shout in unison, startling me into motion.

My hands fly to my face, covering half of it. "Thank you!" My chest heaves, a sign that I was definitely not breathing for a moment there. "What are you both doing here?" I ask, leaning into Ms. Kestrel's hug.

"We're here to celebrate you," she replies sweetly. "Why

else would we be in your kitchen just after sunrise? Everyone knows you're not a morning person."

Tears well in my eyes and threaten to fall down my face as the sentiment of her words, the idea that there are finally more people than just Kaida who want to celebrate me because of who I am, sinks in. Jareth and Kaida wrap around us, and the three of them give me the most uncomfortable group hug I've been pulled into. Kaida doesn't give me time to recover when she releases me before she shoos me out of the kitchen.

I plop down in a dining room chair, the scent of the cake pooling all around me. It's so strong that I wipe my chin more than once, and I'm almost certain drool is pouring down my face as I wait. Famished isn't a word strong enough to describe how I feel once it's finally sat in front of me and my stomach makes a noise so loud, I'm sure they heard it in Smallburrow.

As my friends sing the traditional birthday song to me, a warmth spreads through me by what—and who—I'm surrounded by. The cake tradition has been in place for as long as I've been Kaida's friend. She's never let my birthday go by without baking one, always ensuring I know how cherished I am. When my parents were still alive, she and my mom would wake me up with a song and a slice of cake; even after their death, Kaida has never failed to keep it going.

She refuses to believe me when I say that she is the best gift I could ask for and the light that carries me through the darkest days. The thought of my mother brings a bittersweet smile to my face as memories of birthdays past surface. I stuff the memories down as deep as possible before the emotions flood through me, turning my attention back to those who are with me today. The worst thing that could happen today is for them to see me crying and think that something is wrong or that I don't want them here.

The slice of heaven Kaida places before me is nothing short of a physical representation of her love for me. It's beautiful on the outside, but warm and gooey on the inside. Like everything else she makes, it's addicting, and it takes every ounce of willpower I possess not to devour a third slice before our neighbors leave.

After they promise to return for dinner, they leave, and the house is quiet. I resolve to spend the remainder of the day relaxing in my favorite chair, book in hand. Unfortunately, I have gotten so accustomed to being busy that, by early afternoon, I'm bored and need something for my hands to do. After pacing around the house to the point that Kaida yells at me to "find something to do and get out of her hair," I toss my cloak around my shoulders and wander around the garden, grabbing the medium-sized basket I keep next to the door.

I stop next to the first small plot across from the herb planters and kneel to inspect it. Leaning closer, I wrap my hand around the leafy green top of the carrots and pull them from the ground with ease. Carrots, as well as potatoes and snap peas, have unexpectedly become big sellers at the market in the last week or so, and it has become an unspoken requirement that Number One Booth keep them in stock. With the weather turning cooler, everyone's minds–my own, included–has latched onto it being the perfect weather to incorporate more soup.

A lazy smile turns the corners of my mouth upward as I contemplate how successful Number One Booth has already become in such a short amount of time, and, without my notice, Jareth appears next to me when I turn to go back toward the house.

"Hiya, Eilaen," he says with a wave.

I yelp as I jump, his presence never failing to startle me. Using one of the old elvish curses taught to me by Kaida's grandfather, I face him. "Long time no see, stranger." I brush the dirt from my hands and give him a forced smile while simultaneously willing my thrumming heart to slow down.

He claps before his fingers brush the unruly mop of curls from his eyes, his laughter filling the space around us. "You know I can't stay away from this place for long. Especially not when my two favorite neighbors live here, and they never fail to send me home stuffed and heavier than when I arrived. Not to mention the leftovers I always have for the next day." He clears his throat and looks down nervously. "Besides, it is your birthday today, is it not?"

I nod, leaning to the side slightly and giving him a wary

sideways glance. His hand dives into his pocket, clutching a small box when it appears again. With a sheepish look, he hands it to me. "Well, what kind of friend would I be if I forgot to give you this?"

In my hand is a beautifully wrapped box. The paper around it reminds me of the shade of yellow the sun's rays are when they peek out through the trees in the morning, and the tiny orange bow on top is the color of the sunset. My name has been elegantly penned directly under the bow, and the whole thing is so perfect that it almost pains me to open it. Inside rest three beautiful metal bookmarks, each half the size of my pointer finger, with a blunt hook on top to keep them in place.

Blinking tears away, again, I take a deep breath and look at him. "Jareth. Thank you so much. This was so incredibly thoughtful of you. They're beautiful. I love them!"

"I'm glad. I noticed last week when I was here that your current bookmark is looking well-loved and in need of retirement. I thought you might like some that are more durable and can withstand the life you live now." His eyes dart around, looking everywhere but me, before settling on the ground as he inhales shakily. "I, erm, wanted to ask... Ask you something. But, uh.." His voice falters as if he's struggling to find the words for whatever it is he's trying to say.

I give him a moment, slowly nodding my head in encouragement. "Yes? What is it?" I finally ask. I hate pushing people when they're having a hard time, but not knowing what he wants to say is more nerve-wracking to me than almost anything else I can think of.

"I was wondering if y-," he says in a rush, but is interuppted when Kaida's voice cuts him off.

"It's dinnertime, friends!" she exclaims, standing at the doorway.

I look towards her and wave, indicating that we're coming, and turn back to Jareth, who's looking at the house in horror. "Don't worry, Kaida didn't cook," I reassure him. "Ms. Kestrel came over to help Kaida make supper so that it'll actually be edible. How in this world Kaida was gifted with such an incredible amount of baking magic and not a single ounce of cooking ability, I will never know." Though he doesn't look very convinced, he slowly exhales as if holding a breath. "Now what was it that you were wanting to ask?"

"Oh. It wasn't anything too important. Come on. It's starting to get cold, and I am starved. Is the window open because I can smell whatever Ms. Kestrel cooked, even from all the way over from here!" He awkwardly rambles. He takes off towards the house after grabbing my basket of carrots and, though he's turned where I can't see his face, I swear there's a splash of red staining his fair-skinned cheeks.

He's such an odd bean. I wish I could see what was going on inside his head. It would make being around him so much easier than waiting for him to make his thoughts known.

I have to practically triple the length of my natural stride to catch up with him, and he only slows down when I reach him. Grabbing my arm, he pulls me along as we run together, despite my complaints of not doing cardio on my birthday.

❧❧❧

After two bowls of a hearty potato soup, more fresh bread and cheese than I could ever quantify, and the pumpkin ale Kaida and I have been saving specifically for my birthday, I sit back in my chair and rub my hand over my achingly full belly. Neither Kaida nor I drink ale often, and even with eating, the look she gives me tells me that her head is buzzing just as much as mine is. Still, never one to turn down a good mug of ale, I nod my head when she offers a refill, as does Jareth.

"Hey," she yells, hiccuping. "Who wants to race?"

Jareth's hand instantly flies up as if he's in primary school, and I yell my acceptance to her challenge. "Winner gets to pick who has to clean up! Ms. Kestrel," I ask, leaning towards her. "Will you be the judge? I don't trust these ninny heads."

Ms. Kestrel shakes her head but counts down. "Three, two, one. Go!"

The moment she yells, we throw our heads back and drain our cups as quickly as possible. To everyone's surprise, including my own, I finish first, announcing doing so by slamming my

87

metal mug onto the table. Jareth follows right behind me with Kaida bringing up the rear of the race less than a second later. Kaida joins me as I cheer for my victory, clutching her sides as she cackles when I appoint Jareth to clean up. Beside us, Ms. Kestrel rolls her eyes in what can be described as fit for a grandmother.

As Kaida clears the dishes from the table, I walk with Ms. Kestrel to the door as she prepares to leave for the night. Before stepping outside, she embraces me tightly before gently planting a kiss on my cheek. "Happy birthday, Eilaen, my girl. I am so thankful that it was you who has moved next door to me," she whispers softly as her wrinkled palm pats my cheek.

After giving me another squeeze, I watch her leave, not moving from the doorway until she reaches the end of the pathway and turns towards her house, my fingers tenderly brushing the skin where she kissed. It's a gesture that baffles me. It's strange, yet comforting, and though I wasn't given the chance to know my grandmother, I imagine she would have loved me in all the ways Ms. Kestrel does.

"Aww. Is poor Jaree Bear sad because he has to wash the dishes?" Kaida gleefully taunts, and I walk into the kitchen to see Jerath glaring at her over the stack of dishes next to the sink.

She dances past me, carrying a large metal bowl of scraps for the pigs, still laughing as the door opens and closes. Even with the window closed, I can hear the joyful notes of the song she's singing as she walks in the dark, though there's a pause as she yells "oops" more than once. Jareth hunches over the sink as he cleans the dishes, softly singing an old Fae tune. Intrigued, I move beside him and pick up the dish towel from the counter, drying the dishes after he rinses them, and enjoying the song he's singing.

When he stops, I nod my head towards him. "You have a nice singing voice. I couldn't understand most of the words, but the song sounded lovely."

"Thanks," he mumbles, sliding another bowl into my side of the sink.

Silently, we work side-by-side in a comfortable rhythm, almost as if this is a task we do together nightly. It's nice, I decide, to be able to be in a space where I can be myself with someone other than Kaida. That is, until the last dish is placed in the sink, when he smiles strangely at me. My stomach lurches, flipping in alarm as he leans closer to me.

To my horror, I watch as his eyes close and his lips pucker, and I can't breathe. It's as if the puckering has stolen my breath from me, and it threatens to freeze me in place. Just before his lips meet mine, I finally force myself to move, though it's only enough for him to graze my temple instead of missing me altogether.

His eyes instantly fly open, embarrassment evident in how wide they are. He coughs, clears his throat, and walks away as he rasps a final "happy birthday." He stops moving long enough to bid Kaida a goodnight, and she stands next to me. When the door closes, she looks at me in bewilderment, and I can practically watch the gears turning through her mind as she tries to figure out what happened in the minutes she was gone. I shrug when she raises her brow in question, not knowing how or where to begin with explaining the circumstances around his departure.

The awkward tension in the air combusts as we both erupt into a fit of ale-induced giggles before trailing slowly up the stairs and to their rooms. We finish cleaning the kitchen before turning in for the night, the clock chiming midnight as I hit my bed. Already, the sounds of Kaida's snores drift across the hall and become the background that threatens to soothe me to sleep. My mind refuses to succumb, instead choosing the reel and replaying the events of the night; each spiral begins with the tender gift of affection that Ms. Kestrel gave me and ends with the awkward scene from the kitchen with Jareth.

No matter how hard I try not to, I continue to replay the moments leading up to the moment that I hope won't ruin our friendship. How did I miss that he has unrequited feelings like that for me? Doesn't he see me the way I see him, as a sibling? Obviously not because, even with me being an only child, I know that is not the way one tries to show affection to their sibling.

I shudder, deciding to take a "wait and see" approach to the situation at hand and hope he chooses to do the same. Or maybe he'll just pretend it never happened. I think I can get behind that idea. There's no doubt he's kind and handsome, albeit a tad bit annoying. But I cannot imagine having even the smallest bit of romantic feelings for him, and surprisingly, I want things between the two of us to stay the way they are.

As my thoughts space out in the way that only comes with drifting off to sleep, my final one is that of the family I'm slowly allowing myself to ease into and hoping they feel the same way that I do.

Fruits of Her Labor

I spend the two days following the "event" with my mind replaying the disaster, as well as the unanswered question of why he thought it was a good idea to try without maing sure the feelings were mutual on my end. Thankfully, I can finally move forward when the real threat of winter affecting the garden engrosses me and I remember that I still need to get the farm ready for winter—hopefully before the Autumn Festival, which is barely two weeks away. Suddenly, the answer hits me and I cannot believe it's one I haven't considered until now.

Which is why I'm standing here at the window, waiting for Jareth to appear. I've kept myself as busy as I can today, yet it seems to have made it stretch that much longer. Finally, I see the top of his head appear on our side of the tree marking the halfway point between houses and I run outside to meet him.

"Jareth!" My arms wave frantically over my head in desperation to get his attention as quickly as possible. "I know what I'm about to ask you is potentially the craziest question of my life, but I also know that you're the only one I know that can answer it."

He stops mid-stride and leans back, his brows nearly touching as he cautiously nods. Taking this as my cue to continue, I blurt out my question, my voice so high that I'm practically screaming at him. "What are the chances that someone who wasn't born with an affinity for nature magic can learn to summon and wield it? I guess what I'm asking is if there is any chance at all that I could possibly learn how to use magic on my own to keep the garden going when winter hits?"

He stands in front of me, silent and bewildered as one hand strokes his chin while the other fidgets in his pocket. After taking time to ponder my question, he says "I suppose it would be possible, yes." He pauses, his tone less confident than I want it to be, but not completely lacking hope. "But it would take a lot of work. Daily work. Work that may be really hard, both mentally and physically, if it were to appear at all."

Hope blossoms inside my chest at the possibility, allowing my next question to come more naturally. "Can you teach me?"

My heart beats wildly inside my chest, the blood rushing through it as it thunders in my ears. I wipe the dampness on my palms against my trousers as I wait for his reply.

"I- I can try, I guess," he answers slowly. "Do you have any books on magic? I know your grandparents loved to bring home anything knowledge related."

I shake my head slowly. If they did, I have yet to see it and I've been quite a bit of time in the library as of late. His face brightens and he excitedly exclaims "Wait here. I'll be right back," before turning around and sprinting toward his home.

I stand for what feels like hours, though in reality, I know it's only minutes. I'm rocking on my heels when I spy him jogging around the tree again. In his hand is something small and dark brown, but when he gets closer, I realize it's some kind of book. He stops in front of me, thrusting the small text into my hands as he breathes fast from exertion.

As I inspect it, I notice it's a child's primer on conjuring magic, and surprisingly it's a lot heavier than it appears to be. It smells faintly of old paper, leather, and dust. The cover is green leather that has cracked from age, the golden lettering covering the front mostly worn to nothing. The edges also appear to have once been golden, but like the lettering, the metallic paint has worn away with time, what little bit remains leaving glittering streaks across the tips of my fingers.

I flip through the pages, a jolt of pleasure running through me at the worn illustrations that are now discolored and faded from years gone by. were well worn and the illustrations had grown discolored and faded over the years. I go through it front to back, but when I open it a second time, I see a small detail I missed. In little messy letters is a name.

Jareth

A small squeak leaves me as I look up at my friend. "This was yours when you were a little Fae-ling?"

He smiles softly, his fingers tracing the letters of his name as if recalling the memories connected to the book. 'It was. It's actually one of the last physical reminders of my childhood, at least that I have in my possession. Honestly, though, that's more than likely because it just sits there on a shelf, barely seen and never touched. Maybe it'll be useful for your journey?" He rubs the back of his neck and his eyes dart toward the ground.

I open my mouth to ask about what happened in my kitchen, but close it almost immediately. Instead, I give him a smile before looking at the book again. "When do we start?"

A mischievous grin stretches across his face, transforming him into the Fae she's grown to know. A small flash of worry goes through my body, but before I can ask him again, he's practically dragging me across the yard and to the garden.

"Sit," he demands and yanks me down as he plops onto the ground.

With an "oomph", I sit next to him, my body rigid with the fear of what's to come. He releases me and crosses his legs, holding his hands over the plot of dirt with him palms facing it. "Do everything I do," he says before wriggling his body as if preparing it for something.

Awkwardly, I hold my hands exactly like he has his, and wait for further instruction. I've never seen him before he prepares to use his magic,the day I witnessed it being the one and only time he's had to summon it since I've known him, and there's no feasible way for me to prepare for this lesson. He inhales deeply and holds it long enough that I can count to three before releasing it. "Regardless of someone's race or class, everyone has a tiny spark of magic nestled deep within them. For most, it's so insignificant that it's never noticed, and when ignored, the spark goes permanently dormant, never to be used or acknowledged. For others, the spark nudges them until one day, whether accidentally or on purpose, they conjure it and it flares to life in a way that completely transforms their lives."

"What does that spark feel like?" I ask.

Is it possible that the strange pull inside of me is my spark?

He twists his mouth to the side thoughtfully for a beat before answering. "If I had to describe it, I would say that it's something that is probably different for everyone. For me, it's like the warmth of the sun's rays on a chilly day. Not hot like a fire within the fireplace, but warm like a cup of tea. At first, it was so small, probably the size of a corn kernel if I had to describe it now. But as it grew, it got stronger and larger. Eventually, I was able to summon it effortlessly instead of having to coax it out of hiding. Now, it doesn't feel like the rays of the sun, but instead it almost transforms me into the sun. Does that make sense?"

I nod. "It does."

His explanation inspires the single most beautiful imagery to form inside of me, and I'm slightly taken aback by how profound he can be when necessary. When he closes his eyes, I do the same and try to focus on searching for a small spark of something, anything, deep within me. We work at it for quite awhile, though none of my attempts are successful.

After a while, we take a break, and when I growl in frustration at my failure, he gently reminds me that I shouldn't feel defeated. "Today is the first day of your journey, Eilaen. There's nothing to suggest that it would have appeared, especially after being hidden for so many years. Let's go inside and see what Kaida has whipped up. I am famished!"

Reluctantly, I agree and, after a cup of tea and a piece of cinnamon apple bread, we prepare to head back to the garden.

"Why do you have to be outside for all of this?" Kaida asks, following us to the door.

In response, Jareth looks at her with one brow raised and a smirk on his face. "Where else would you expect to have the best success with nature magic than sitting, you know, in nature?"

She looks at me like he's speaking another language, mouthing if he's been smoking his pipe today. I shrug as I give her a little wave and follow him. As I lower myself to the ground,

I sit on the crunchy brown grass that's covering the yard and close my eyes again.

Taking a deep breath, I will my body to relax and search again for the small spark that I hope is hidden within me, though that hope isn't nearly as bright as it had been when I first sought Jareth out this morning.

By the end of the day, I am thoroughly exhausted and my body aches as if I've been trampled by a herd of rowdy farm animals. Despite the many hours spent on finding it, only one attempt had been successful enough for me to grasp my spark. I held it for only a moment before it got away, and what should have been satisfaction that it's possible is only frustration that I'll be going to bed tonight after a long day of struggling, and I have next to nothing to show for it.

Before leaving, Jareth walks me to the door and places his hand on my shoulder. "We'll get you there," he says encouragingly. "The fact that you have been able to find it at all means that your chances for harnessing the magic inside of you are better than we both thought they'd be. I'll see you in the morning when you're done with chores, and we'll try again, okay?

I groan at the idea of doing this again tomorrow, but I haven't forgotten that he's working with me because I promised I would put in the work. To not do so would make me a liar, and I, Eilaen Mapleground, am the exact opposite of that. Once his footsteps are faded enough for me to no longer hear them, I hurriedly search through the rows of plants and look for anything needing to be harvested. I have to have something to take to the market this week and I can't expect Kaida to pick up my slack because I want to go on what could be a goose chase for magic. That wouldn't be fair or kind to her, especially after she's already done so much for me.

Though I have already learned so much in regards to running a farm, there are still so many things I'm still confused about. Most of these questions revolve around anything that grows beneath the dirt.

How do I know root plants are ready for harvest without pulling them too early? How do I know I waited too long? It all boils down to a guessing game at this point and it's one I hate playing.

None of the fruit bearing plants are currently producing any fruit, which one would correctly expect as winter is only two days away, and I make a mental note to come back tomorrow to prune the tree limbs like the book I have been reading suggests. Now I waste no time in moving to the herb boxes, their scents mingling deliciously as I take in a deep breath. The peaceful sensation they bring me relaxes my mind in ways very few things can, and my muscles loosen in response.

Knowing everything has been harvested, I connect the weird rubber tube to the sprinkler that Jareth created, and use it to water the garden thoroughly. Though I'm still unsure how it works, I am thankful for the contraption allowing the water to flow freely throughout a wider area. The ground is much drier than it should be due to the lack of rain, and we would be struggling without it.

Satisfied that everything is sufficiently hydrated, I turn the water off at it's source and collect the baskets of produce from my harvest. As I drift closer to the house, I fall into a daydream, imagining what it would be like if I had the ability to tend to the garden with magic instead of the simple work I do now. *What would it be like to nurture the plants on a whim with nothing more than my fingertips?*

The fantasy I create keeps me sufficiently occupied as I whip up a simple chicken noodle soup for supper, and is only interrupted by my conversation with Kaida as we eat and clean the kitchen for the night. Even as I sleep, the dream continues with the manifestation of a small spark that grows more the longer I spend in this little world I've conjured within my imagination.

The sensation of warmth persists throughout the night, and when I wake, I am invigorated from the hope it's given me. I leap from my bed and quickly dress before running out the door. Hurriedly, I complete my chores and don't even grumble when I have to corral an extremely mischievous Tillard back into his pen. I even manage to only threaten him once, calling him naughty before threatening to turn him into stew if he didn't stay put; this is also done only after I close him in his pen and no longer have to chase him around the garden, the big meathead.

Thankfully, the cows are much ricer to me, cooperating when I move them as needed to tend to them. Though, it doesn't escape me that both Brenda and Bessie seem extra perturbed when I accidentally swap their names around, something I've been doing much better about. To be fair, it's still incredibly difficult to differentiate between the two when they're standing side by side.

I chastise myself for working too quickly after I finish the chores and take the eggs and milk inside. I'm stuck waiting for Jareth to show up, something he typically does around the time I finish when I move normally. chores were finished and the eggs and milk had been dropped off in the kitchen, she waited patiently until Jareth arrived. Finally, he meanders down the path and, when he sees me waving, heads over to where I sit in the same spot as yesterday.

Without waiting for his instructions, I repeat the same string of movements as before, the sensation of warm spreading through me more noticeable today. I grasp it, digging deeper into myself, though not as deep as I have been expecting to. Even with having to work to get to it, I'm still able to grab and hold it, almost as if it's become more tangible within me.

My eyes fly open. "I did it!" I yell. "I could feel it. I could see it. I couldn't keep hold of it, but I held it. Jareth, I held it!"

He pulls me to my feet and together, we jump up and down in excitement. After we calm down and sit back on the ground, I work to summon it again. It doesn't happen as easily as last time, but I don't care because I can say I've done it twice in a row. The warmth it gives me seeps into my bones comfortingly, as if this magic is a blanket on a cool evening under the stars.

The more we practice, the more hope flows through me and gives me the confidence to trust the process as it unfolds instead of rushing through it. By the end of the day, I'm still unable to summon it with as much ease as Jareth, but I refuse to be disappointed in myself. Today wasn't perfect, but it wasn't a failure either. It was progress. Inside of me is a living spark, growing with determination as I strive to learn everything I can about it.

This magic is something I wish to wield flawlessly, and I want to be able to do so in the event the unthinkable happens and the garden fails overnight as winter approaches.

My body is more worn down than yesterday, the physical drain of the magic more noticeable, and instead of standing at the stove to cook dinner, I put together a sample board. I stack it high with dried meats, cheeses, the few remaining berries on the counter, and a handful of thin wafers that Kaida accidentally created from an experiment gone wrong.

In my exhaustion, I forget to return to the garden to harvest the items for tomorrow, deciding to rise early tomorrow to do so before we leave. The last thought I have before slipping into a deep sleep is of how incredible today was and how I cannot wait for more to come.

Eilaen and the No Good, Terribly Difficult Day

I spend hours upon hours immersing myself in learning all that I can about magic over the next week, desperate to soak in all I can about the abilities I'm manifesting. Though I've gotten my hands to glow consistently, that's been the farthest I've gotten. I can sense the spark as it grows into a flame as I practice, and it no longer shrinks when I release it. Yet I still cannot identify the most efficient way to coax it out further. It comes as no surprise, then, that I've been more drained than I had previously considered plausible.

With two weekends to go until the Autumn Festival, time passes by faster than I thought possible, and, not for the first time, the fear of my goal being unattainable has me clutching my chest. Winter is just around the corner, the chill in the mornings and evenings a daily reminder of my original deadline, and I respond by using my frustration to push harder. All I want is for the garden to thrive, even with snow on the ground. If I have this magic inside of me, there is no reason why this shouldn't be possible. The people of Smallburrow have been nothing but kind and welcoming to Kaida and me, and all I want to do is give them the same kindness by ensuring their bellies are full of nutritious produce all winter long.

Is that really too much for one halfling to ask for?

While dreaming, I knew today wasn't going to go my way, and looking back, I'm not sure why I didn't simply stay in bed.

From the moment my fat, hairy feet touch the cool stone floor, unease sweeps through me before settling in my gut like a rock. These suspicions are further founded when I try to leave the house to tend to the animals, and cannot get the door open. As if it has a will of its own, it's refusing to budge at all.

What is going on? I cock my head to the side to see if there's something I'm missing, but nothing is blocking it from opening. The knob twists when I move it, so it's not locked. Nothing appears to be between the door and the frame on any side. Maybe it just needs some percussive persuasion.

Rearing my leg back, I channel every ounce of sourness left from yesterday's failures and kick the wooden slab as hard as I can. Nothing happens, and I have nothing to show for my efforts other than my sore pride and throbbing red toes; the latter of which I learn of after I storm towards the den so I can further contemplate any other options I may have. It's going to be a real problem if we cannot get the door open, seeing as it's the only entrance. This is also probably the worst time to realize how inconvenient it is to have one way in and one way out.

"Why did you think one door would be enough?" I ask, looking up as if waiting for my grandparents to answer.

Frustration rolls through me, and it takes half a dozen more attempts before the final idea comes to mind. I sigh deeply, resigning myself to the fact that there truly isn't any other way for me to get out. I'm going to have to climb through the window over the sink and hope with all that I am that I don't die from falling out of it.

Awkwardly, I hobble through the dining room, selecting the closest chair I can grab, and tug it with me to the kitchen. Whoever carved these chose a wood so heavy that it takes some effort on my part to get it close to my destination, and that's even after I stop once to catch my breath.

Is it heavy or am I just that unfit, I ask myself, landing on the chair simply being heavier than expected. As I pass the island, I sight the backless stool Kaida uses and immediately hate myself for not considering the stool before the thing I'm still dragging.

"Maybe there's an enchantment that keeps it from tipping over, and that's why it's so heavy," I whisper, wheezing between words as I slide it next to the sink.

Catching my breath once again, I stand in the seat and hoist myself up onto the counter top. A step to my right reveals the grave error from last night: a bowlful of water left for "later" because I was too lazy to wash it last night. The icy water splashes me, covering my ankle and foot.

Great, now one foot is practically numb, and the other is throbbing so much, I can scarcely think. Can this get any worse?

Wrong thing to say, because, though my next step to the side is smooth, the window opens with more ease than anticipated, and I fall headfirst into the large pot of basil and thyme that rests underneath it on the outside.

A scream rips from me as I scramble to right myself. "Kaida can do this next time, because I am not doing it. I already refuse."

As if summoned, her voice drifts through the window. "Ellie, where are you?" Her head peeks out as she sticks it out, concern covering her face. "What are you doing?"

I throw a glare her way. "I'm just sitting here, Kaida. What does it look like I'm doing? Sleeping?"

Her brow furrows. "You don't have to be a rude ninny, ya know," she replies, her arms folding across her chest.

"I know," I answer reluctantly. "I'm sorry. It's just already proving to be a long day, and it's only just begun. The door is stuck, and I cannot get it to open." I launch into detail of what's happened between my rising from bed and her finding me, choosing to ignore the way her hands fly to cover her mouth.

Once I'm done, she shakes her head. "Of all the messes to get into, Eilaen Mapleground, this has to be the pickliest. Can you get out of the pot?"

I wiggle, my twisted figure struggling to get itself into one direction, and when I finally accomplish it, I fall out of the pot and hit the ground with a thud. Before worrying about myself, I look over the herbs and wince as I see how terribly I've flattened them.

Kaida's face pinches when she sees them, the expression quickly fading. "Don't worry, Ellie. Jareth can fix 'em when he gets here."

I grunt and stomp away, yelling that I'll be in the barn if she needs me. Two steps later, and my feet find the largest mud puddle I've ever seen. Without anything to hold onto, I slip in the mud, which does nothing but further frustrate me to the point of screaming.

Covered head to toe in the gritty muck, I storm into the barn and slam the door open. The cows and pigs scatter, all having been terrified by the crash. I run to close it, but before I can grasp the handle, the five animals bolt outside, and I have to launch myself sideways to avoid being trampled.

Tears sting my eyes as I let out a cry of exasperation, and I run around the yard to corral four of the five animals I've been chasing. The only one left? Tillard.

"Please, Tillard," I beg, my voice weary as I plead with him. "Please cooperate and go inside. I promise I won't yell at you for the rest of the week. I'll give you extra scraps. I'll give you anything you want if you will just go back inside." I fall to my knees in a hopeful attempt to show him how sincere I am, and when he saunters forward, a weight lifts from my chest.

Unfortunately, the weight then crashes down even harder when he turns around and runs in the opposite direction. "You're a dead pig trotting, Tillard!" I scream, throwing my hands up and trudging towards the chicken coop.

My luck only trends downwards as the rooster and two of the three hens try to trip me in their desperation to escape the coop, causing me to drop six of the eggs I'm juggling.

Beaten, both emotionally and physically, I slowly make my way around the garden and towards the house. Before trying to open it, I look over every inch of it as I try to locate the issue. Like before, it doesn't seem as if anything is wrong with it. My hand wraps around the knob and, assuming it's not going to budge without force, I throw my entire body into it. I instantly learn what people say about not making assumptions when it flies open as if nothing has been wrong, and I, yet again, land on my face.

Scrambling to my feet, I stand in the entryway covered in mud, grass, and egg yolk, crying to Kaida when she comes to investigate the source of the noise. "I'd ask if today could get any worse," I sob, tears and snot rubbing down my face. "But the last time I asked myself that, it did."

Comforting me from a distance, she encourages me to get into the bath and sit until today's frustrations have melted away. So I do, I sit in the tub until the water is muddy before draining it. Then, I fill the basin up again and sit until it's too cold to manage anymore. By the time my feet touch the bottom step, I'm able to breathe easier than at any other point today.

Refreshed, I'm now ready to cuddle up on the couch with a hot cup of tea and something cozy to eat. "Good day, Eilaen," a familiar male voice says, and though I shouldn't be, I'm gobsmacked to find Jareth sitting on the sofa.

His smile hints that he was the sole witness to this morning's shenanigans, resurrecting the scowl I worked so hard to rid myself of. "Oh, now you're here. Of course you are. Why am I surprised to see that you're here when I don't need you to be? It's so utterly convenient on your part to not be needed when around, isn't it?"

An amused look sweeps across his face, and he fails to stifle his laughter. "I am, indeed. Have you had an interesting day today, then?" His grin is full of mischief as if he's hiding something.

Yep, I think it's safe to say he witnessed every single moment of what I've been through today.

Saving the day–and probably Jareth's life–Kaida sweeps into the room with a cup of tea in one hand and a fresh-baked cinnamon roll in the other. After placing them on the table next to my chair, she plops down into her own chair before turning to scold Jareth. "Oh, you. Behave. Didn't I already tell you she has had a ridiculously difficult day today?"

Before he can answer her question, I round on him. "How's my day been so far? Well, let me tell you about the adventure I've been on today, and all before lunchtime at that. It started with me struggling because the only door that leads out of the house got stuck. For no reason whatsoever. Then, in my attempt to make it outside, I fell out the window, where I flattened out an entire container of herbs. Herbs that you are going to need to fix, by the way, friend." I stop speaking long enough to take a breath, and then continue.

"That led to me falling into the biggest mud puddle I've come across in my not-so-long life. I also managed to scare the cows and pigs, and all five of them escaped. I finally corralled most of them back inside, only to go into the coop where the chickens tried to murder me, covering me in egg goo. Oh, and I'm fairly certain Tillard is still at large. So, yes, I would say my day has been *rather* adventurous." His face drains of color at the glare that enunciates my final word, and I force myself to pop another bite of my cinnamon roll into my mouth before I can yell at him some more.

"If I didn't know better, my Ellie dear, I'd say that you are rather cranky, though I wouldn't possibly know why." Kaida giggles, clapping her flour-coated hands towards me.

I glare at her, but Jareth interrupts me when I try to deny her statement. "What happened to the door? It opened fine whenever I came in."

I roll my eyes. "I dunno, Jareth. If I knew that, then I *probably* wouldn't have had to climb out the window. I mean, that makes sense, right? Or did you miss the *entire* story of what happened this morning? Here's the shortened version for better comprehension. I twisted the doorknob and tried to open it. It refused to open. Kicking it did absolutely nothing other than hurt my toe, and because of all of that, I thought I could climb out the window. All that was accomplished was me falling out of it and flattening my herbs. Does this honestly sound like something I would do for fun now?" I huff before taking a deep breath and will myself to calm down.

"Of course it doesn't. Well, now that the door situation has sorted itself out, after you're done eating, we'll go and get the herbs cared for and then try to convince Tillard that he wants to be with Lottle and Benji." The sympathetic smile he throws my way reminds me genuinely does care, which helps to thaw my frosty mood. He smiled at Eilaen, effectively thawing her frosty mood.

"The meathead is still running around?" I ask through a mouthful of cinnamon roll.

"Yep. Running around the farm like the hairy pink menace that we all know he is. I didn't see the mess you made while I was out there, but I did fix some of the other plants that he'd trampled." He slaps his leg and laughs. "Well, I'll ya what, that pig better be careful, or he'll end up as the main course at this year's Winter Feast."

His joke is the final shove I need to get rid of my bad mood, and as I sit laughing with my friends, the crankiness and frustration melt from my body.

Every day, I have more reason to be thankful for the two incredible beings beside me, as well as the one not here. We sit a while longer, avoiding the chase we know is coming by eating cinnamon rolls with Kaida and Jareth bantering back and forth. Only once the food is gone and the icing has been cleaned from our fingers are we ready to venture forth to capture our porky nemesis.

Kaida is the first to find him, immediately doing so after rounding the house. He's in his favorite spot between the garden and the animal enclosures. As if knowing what we're coming to do, he sits and watches warily as we close in on him. Before we get farther than the halfway point, he looks at me one more time before taking off, squealing loudly as he runs.

Around and around, the three of us run, attempting every maneuver we can conjure to outsmart and outrun him.

"Are you playing some kind of sick game with us?" Kaida screams before launching herself at him, her hand grazing his side as she hits the ground.

The noise he utters in reply is one of wicked glee, and he practically smirks at us with humor in his eyes that grows with each failed attempt to grab him. Finally, we're successful, though I have a sneaking suspicion it only happens because he got tired of being chased around. Once he's back where he belongs, the three of us drop onto the grass.

"I'm so done with him," I say, my chest heaving.

Jareth gives a noise that I take as him agreeing with me, and Kaida replies with "yep. Same."

"No more today," I beg. "I just want to stay inside and do nothing."

Sitting up, Jareth nods. "I second that."

"I third it," Kaida agrees, pushing herself up to stand.

We trudge back inside, Jareth draping himself across the sofa while Kaida drops down into her chair, and I follow, dropping down into mine. I snuggle deep under my favorite blanket, grateful that tomorrow isn't a market day. I flip through the pages to find my place in my favorite book, *Back and Forth Again: A Halfling's Trip with Twelve Dwarves and a Wizard*, not caring to pay attention to the rest of the day as it passes by.

Between the events of this morning, chasing Tillard, and the crackling of the fire, I eventually succumb to my heavy eyelids and fall into a nap, dreaming of a day when I will no longer be subjected to chasing that stupid pig around the farm.

The Magic of Smallburrow

To pay him back for the help he gave us with pig wrangling, Kaida, and I both promise to help Jareth with preparations for the Autumn Festival. To say we are currently immersed in them is an understatement, to put it mildly. Upon learning about our promise, Ms. Kestrel has ensured that we've been placed in areas where we can be the most beneficial, stressing the importance of our involvement in the community event to the fullest extent possible.

"As the newest members of the community, as well as the current owners of Number One Booth, you must allow yourselves to become a vital beat within the heart of Smallburrow," Ms. Kestrel stated, and has frequently reminded us of.

Thankfully, one of the accommodations Smallburrow has for festival preparation is that the market closes its doors for the length of the two weekends set before the grand opening. Unsurprisingly, Kaida is immediately welcomed by the decorating committee, courtesy of Ural's demands, whereas I'm right at home as I assist Ms. Kestrel with the tasks involved in organizing both the baking competition and the information for the contestants who have placed their entries into it.

Organization and administrative tasks are areas where I excel, finding them to be much more enjoyable to me than those required for 90% of the other committees. When it's time for lunch, I wander around as I search Market Square for Kaida, amazed at how quickly our little town is at pulling something together when the event is so large-scale.

The Autumn Festival is quickly becoming much grander than anything I've been part of, and I'd be lying if I were to say I'm not excited.

As I pass booth after booth, I watch the merchants work on their specialty items while simultaneously restocking the everyday things they need for when the market opens next week. It doesn't take long before I'm struck with the realization that I've truly come to love both the town and its residents. I've learned the names of most everyone, and I can even tell you where the majority of them live. I know what someone wants without them speaking their order, regardless of who it is.

I laugh genuinely and smile as I interact with them, and for the first time, I am completely comfortable in my own skin. Back in Galbassi, I never got involved in the community out of fear for how others would treat me when I displayed any eccentricities. But *here*? Here in Smallburrow, it's not something that crosses my mind anymore.

Here in Smallburrow, it's different. All of it. My life, the people, the town. I finally know what it means to have a place within my community, and for the first time, I fit in because of who I am, not who I pretend to be.

The magic within me warms as if ignited by the remembrance of my purpose, reminding me it's still there. I am so close to being able to use it that I can practically taste it, comforted by the way it soothes me when it rises to the palms of my hands. Jareth is convinced it's going to manifest any day now, and because of his encouragement, I almost believe that it's possible. I want it to be possible, though I'm also content knowing I'm simply waiting for the right thing to bring it out.

When I finally see Kaida, she's standing in front of an unoccupied building that borders the limits of Market District. Not wanting to interrupt her in whatever she's thinking, I step up beside her as quietly as I can, looking from her to the building and then back to her before instinctively closing my eyes.

In the silence, I can almost imagine the dreams Kaida has, the sounds and smells so strong, I swear they'll truly exist if I were to open my eyes. I'm so wrapped up in my own imagination that I'm startled when she whispers, "It's perfect."

Though I'm unsure as to whether her words are for me or for herself, I grab her hand. "It is, isn't it? When the Autumn Festival is over, we'll work to get it for you, Kai," I promise. "Together."

"Together," Kaida repeats as she opens her eyes and looks at me with a broad smile. "Ready for some sweet treats and good eats?"

My smile matching hers, I nod enthusiastically. "Yes!" I exclaim, my stomach growling audibly as if it's agreeing with me.

Arm in arm, we walk back to the wagon together, ready to head home. As we ride, we chatter about the things we've done and still need to do before the festival next weekend. The atmosphere around us has changed, the nip in the air reminding us to enjoy autumn while we can, as well as to remember to celebrate its ending with the upcoming event.

In detail, Kaida gushes about how much she's learning, as well as how much work goes into decorating a town-wide festival. "I never knew it was such an ordeal," she remarks, her cheeks flushed from her excitement. "There are costumes to make and structures we still need to build. Not to mention the caterers that need to be hired for the food, as well as waiting for the blacksmith to get back to us on a design for the prize for the winner of the maze. Urzal even hired a troop of gardener gnomes who will be designing and constructing the maze this year! Apparently, the design is going to be kept secret to prevent anyone from cheating. Only Urzal and the mayor will know the path to winning." Her hands cover her cheeks, and she squeals, unable to hold it in any longer.

In return, I tell her about the ins and outs of the baking competition. "Kai, it's unlike anything you've ever taken part in. I think every single home baker in town has signed up to contribute something to the sale, so there will still be a ton of stuff there, even though you're one of seven contestants in the competition itself."

"Who am I going up against? Come on, tell me. Tell me!" She grabs my shoulders and shakes me gently, her green eyes wide.

I wiggle out of her grasp, laughing. "You know I won't tell you. Don't even pretend to be offended, Kaida Louise. I know you better than that. You thrive on the idea of winning, and not knowing who you're competing against is only fuel to your fire."

She slides closer to me, and her tone is playful. "If you don't tell me, Eilaen Mapleground, I promise I will knock you out of your seat the moment we pull onto the farm." She doesn't finish her sentence before her laughter starts, and by the time we arrive home, we've both practically dissolved into a puddle of giggles and tears.

I jump out when we stop, unhitching Mabel from the wagon, which stays in front so we can load it before going to the market. As I lead the horse to the back, Kaida yells that she's heading inside to throw a snack together, and the door closes loud enough that I can hear it, even from behind the house.

After I tend to Mabel, I cautiously step towards the garden, biting my lip in contemplation. I stop, trying to convince myself to change my mind, but moves closer to the small plot anyway. I kneel beside the carrots, still cozily rooted in the ground, and inhale a breath that's as shaky as my extended hands as my palms hover over the green sprigs that make the tops. Eyes closed, I reach deep inside of me and pull on the ball of magic. A shiver runs through me, leaving goose pimples across my skin as it rolls down my spine from the flowing of the magic. Through my eyelids, I see a blinding light as an unknown sensation surges through me and onto the ground.

I shout in excitement when I open my eyes to find my palms still lit by the strange light, bursting with joy when I notice the warmth it's emitting is exactly as Jareth had described it the day this all started. Without my full attention on it, the magic goes back into hiding, and the light snuffs itself out. I hurriedly pluck the carrots out of the ground, noting their larger-than-typical size, and run into the house.

"Kaida," I scream, almost tripping over my feet. "Kaida Louise, I did it. I did it!"

With her hands covered in dough, she looks up, doing a double-take when she sees what all the fuss is about. "Those are huge, Eilaen. You did that?"

I nod, unable to speak. The carrots are three times the size of the ones I harvested two days ago, the only difference between those and the ones in my hands being my magic. It takes her a moment to process what I'm showing her, but as soon as it does, she's screaming, and dough is slinging everywhere. Her sticky hands clutch mine, and we jump up and down, neither of us able to stay still.

"Is Jareth coming to dinner tonight?" Kaida shouts.

"I don't know, but I hope so," I yell back.

And for the first time since knowing him, I'm desperate for him to pop up out of nowhere so I can show him the extraordinary miracle I've magicked out of nothing but a seed and belief in myself. Thankfully, he arrives not too much later, and it takes every ounce of patience I possess not to drag him into the garden when he walks through the door. Kaida and I pass glances as we eat, the two of us shoveling our food into our mouths with impressive speed.

The excitement is almost too much to bear, and when he's done eating, I have to take a deep breath to prevent myself from shouting at him. "You two go outside. I'll wash the dishes," Kaida says, practically shoving him out of his chair.

"Uh, okay?" he says, a confused look pinching his face.

I tug his arm. "I just need you to trust me. Come on!"

We run, if one could call it that, with how he's practically limping to keep up with my speed, but he stays quiet until we reach our destination. "Okay, Eilaen. What is going on? You and Kaida have been acting odder than usual since I got here, and that's honestly saying something because you two are incredibly odd. What's the secret?" he demands, crossing his arms across his chest as he looks down at me.

"Oh, spectacular Fae Master of mine. I want to show you this!" I reply, throwing my hands out so I can repeat the process from earlier.

Palms hovering over the cabbage, I close my eyes and draw out the magic within me again. This time, my eyes stay closed when my hands grow warm, and the shiver going down my back isn't as violent as before. When I open my eyes, I see the astonished expression on Jareth's face as he watches the tiny ball of cabbage double in size before him, then triple in size, before it stops after it's four times its normal mass. My smile is so large, it's making my face ache, but it slowly falters as he remains quiet. As I wait for him to say something, anything, I bite into my lower lip. Then it hits me. *I've done something wrong.*

"Is everything... Okay? Did I mess up? Oh, I did, didn't I? I did something wrong. I knew it! Are we going to die? Did I just poison our food? Oh no. We're going to die, and it's going to be all my fault." I know I'm rambling, probably sounding rabid, but I can't make myself shut up.

"It really would be my luck that I finally get this to work, and I've messed everything up without knowing how I did it. Oh my goodness, me. I'm going to end up killing everyone in Smallburrow. Okay, no big deal. I'll just chop my hands off. No hands means no magic. Now, how do I cut off the second hand if it's my only hand? I can't pull Kaida into this..." Sweat drips down my face as I continue to spiral. Finally, he looks at me, and I'm flabbergasted when I notice he's not angry.

No, instead of a scowl, he's smiling, and he looks... Proud? Proud of me?

"El, can you please just shut your mouth? Just for a moment, so I can speak?" Jareth asks, prompting me to instantly close my mouth and stop speaking. "Thank you. Now, I need you to know that you, my dear friend, are incredible. You did not mess anything up or do anything wrong, and no, we're not going to die." The more of my rabid questions he answers, the harder he fights to stifle his laughter before eventually, he can't contain it. He laughs so hard that he's crying, fat tears roll down his cheeks with each shake of his body.

Embarrassment covers me in shame at his reaction until I'm struck with the idea that I probably really do sound as ridiculous as I think I do. I look at him, trying to tell him I'm sorry for being a basket case, but when I see how hard he's working to stay put together, I explode into a fit of my own. My body wracks with laughter to the point that my muscles are contracting, and I have to bend over and clutch my stomach muscles when they get tired and achy.

I barely get myself calmed down when I look over to see Jareth lying in the yard. He must have laughed so hard he fell over, and the sight has me combusting all over again. By the time Kaida comes outside to fetch us, we're lying in the grass, side by side. Our faces are both damp from crying, and we both release exhausted sighs, now tired from our excitement.

She stands over us, shaking her head. "If you younglings are done acting like geese, I have treats in the den to celebrate Eilaen's new ability! Come on, because I promise you that I will eat the entire platter of apple cinnamon scones by myself. This new recipe I've made is incredible. So incredible, in fact, that I almost didn't even come out to share."

Without bothering to see if we follow, she gracefully steps over us and returns to the house, leaving the door open to draw us in with her.

The Wrong Side of the Pig Pen

He hates me. I've been hoping it wasn't the case, but the unfortunate new game Tillard plays with me every morning can only be fueled by two things: hatred and spite. I do not wish to participate, nor do I appreciate him practically forcing me to do so. Nothing about it is amusing in the slightest, and if Kaida would allow me to, I can say with certainty that I would be just fine to get rid of him.

During this game, which apparently can only take place in the mornings, I walk outside only to find that he has either caused a scene inside the barn or has escaped it. So far, the results are tied with two mornings in the barn and two mornings in the yard. The first morning, before it can be labeled an official game of Tillard proportions, I slip into the barn where I am immediately confronted by irate cows that took an entire day to calm down. The next morning, I'm almost trampled as Tillard chases his four barn-mates around the farm. The third and fourth mornings are each a variation of days one and two, respectively.

However, today is day five, and it's suspiciously quiet when I wake. I have to be sure not to let my guard down as I walk outside, or else I won't be able to keep it up whenever I approach the barn; this is something Tillard has learned over the last several weeks.

Cautiously, I creep toward the barn. My eyes dart across the field so he doesn't get the chance to best me. Dread sinks into me more with each step, the silence unnerving.

It's as if he has completely disappeared. There's nothing to suggest he's lurking anywhere on the farm.

Strangely optimistic, I drag the barn door open slowly, hoping that the creaking of its hinges doesn't summon him from wherever it is he's gone to. Like magic, he rips through the space before me, barrels through the door, and knocks me flat on my back.

"Tillard!" I scream, slamming the door closed and sending the cows into another frenzy.

My hands rub their necks as I attempt to soothe them, my soft words and hushed tones also working on myself. When they're sufficiently steady, I grab the milk pail and drag the stool across the floor to where Bessie stands and speak to her as if she'll answer. "Something has got to be done about that menacing pig, Bessie. I don't know what that should be, but something has got to give before he kills some poor, unsuspecting soul."

Reluctantly, I finish tending the animals and set off on my next task–finding the meathead. He's going to destroy my farm, and I honestly don't think I'll be able to stop him from doing so. His vanishing act is perplexing, baffling me more as I look for him.

The vegetables that he loves to romp all over have been left untouched, and the herbs and fruit bushes are unscathed. There are no new holes in the yard, nothing has been destroyed. Everything is as it should be, and while that should bring me comfort, it only covers me with dread from head to toe.

Pretending to take the absence as a gift, I open the door with the intention of taking the milk and eggs into the kitchen. "Kai," I yell, kicking my boots off. "I have to tell you about this morning. Ya know, it's the strangest thing. Tillard has just va-." I'm interrupted by the sounds of Kaida screaming in frustration, a pig snorting furiously, and the banging of metal pans as the crash to the kitchen floor.

The items in my hands forgotten, I run to the kitchen where I'm met with a sight one would only think to find within the pages of a book: Tillard running away as Kaida chases him around the room. White puffs of flour cloud the air, partially obstructing my vision. My body chooses this moment to react as if frozen, my feet cemented to the floor. Kaida chases him in circles, wildly swinging a broom handle in the air and striking towards him violently. I had no plan when I woke this morning, but this isn't something I would have thought should go on my to-do list.

I'm unable to process the sight of her chasing this big, pink, hairy lard of a pig, and I stand, gawking at them as he evades her with a nimbleness I never could have predicted a pig would possess.

The heated glare Kaida gives me finally spurs me into action as she yells at me, the fury in her voice unlike any I've heard her use in the lifetime I've known her. "Eilaen Amorah Mapleground, if you do not help me get this thing out of this kitchen, I will smack you with this broomstick! Please hurry before he-" she begs through gritted teeth, but it's too late. Her plea is cut short by the stack of dirty metal dishes clanging on the floor.

It all happens so quickly that neither of us is able to react in time. Tillard, in his haste to get away from Kaida, knocks the broom from her hands, where it then hits the edge of all four cooling racks holding cookies, which then creates a domino effect as they knock into stacks and stacks of treats, pies, and cakes. In the blink of an eye, every item that Kaida has painstakingly created this week is on the floor, and before she can beg him not to, Tillard shoves his big, hairy, pink nose into the center of it all, rutting it against the floor.

He gobbles down as much as he can in the span of two breaths, and I can only assume it's because he knows Kaida is out for blood. A furious sob rips from her as she watches him devour hours upon hours of hard work, her normally perky face now angry and tomato red.

Before she can, I charge towards him when my foot stomps into a puddle of melted butter next to the island, which launches me forward. Though I attempt to regain my footing, I'm unsuccessful. My arms flail beside me as I fall forward and, to my horror, land right on top of my nemesis. He gives me enough time to wrap my arms around his fat neck before propelling us towards the door. The squeal of terror I release is otherworldly, and I swear my life flashes before my eyes as we crash through the den.

"Tillard!" I cry, trying to get his attention and, hopefully, bring him to a stop. The upper half of my arms both tingle as the blood in them is slowing down due to being constricted from holding him so tightly.

"Stop! Stop running, you useless, bloody, beast of a menace. I swear I will make sure you are the first little piggy I send to the market, and probably the last. A punishment fit only for you." My threats and screams are ignored, and he continues running through the house.

Somehow always one to be the hero, Jareth appears. It flies open just before we can crash into it, and we come to a sudden stop. I stiffly peel my arms away from Tillard, but only after I'm certain that Jareth has a good grasp on him; this experience is not something I ever want to repeat.

Ever.

He doesn't skip a beat before saying, "You know, if you needed help rounding him up, all you had to do was let me know. You didn't have to ride him through the house like a pony."

I stare at him, mouth gaping wide, flabbergasted. "Why are you even here?" I can't be mad at him, even though I give a half-hearted attempt at a scowl. My legs hold me up, shaking. Regardless, I'm just happy to no longer be wrapped around the fat, round, hairy pig that now stood in front of her.

"I told Kaida that I'd be over to help her package up everything for the competition and bake sale tomorrow. I figured she needed an extra set of hands. And by the sounds I heard outside and the ones I'm hearing now, I think I was right," he replies, grunting as Tillard tries to get away. Hearing the old elvish curses coming from the kitchen, he winces. "I'll just... I'll just take him outside."

"Yeah, I'd appreciate that. If he misbehaves one more time, I'm pretty sure Kaida herself will ensure he's donated to the Winter Feast this year," I reply, flinching at the unmistakable sounds of Kaida throwing things from the kitchen.

He waits until I hand him a rope and, once we both see that it's tightly tied around him, Jareth leads him outside to the pen while I turn to make my way back to Kaida. Looking around now, the room is in even more frightful a state than I had realized it to be before riding Tillard. I clear my throat and look at Kaida, ignoring it for the moment. I need to know every detail, beginning to end, of how we ended up with a pig in the kitchen. "Kai. How- how did this happen?"

Tillard's Series of Unfortunate Events

Tear-soaked lashes blink as she looks up from the mashing of baked goods crumbled and smeared across the floor, her eyes shining with tears still unshed.

"There was a knock at the d-door. I just, ya know, assumed it was y-you and that your hands were full because you had been outside for awhile. Y'know? It happens like that s-s-sometimes when you've been to the g-g-garden an-and the barn before coming back into the house. But when I opened the door, it wasn't you. I mean, of course, it wasn't you. Obviously, it wasn't because you didn't get here until after that." She pauses long enough to wipe the snot dripping from her nose with the corner of her apron and then continues.

"It was that stupid pig that acts like he owns the entire blasted farm or something. If I didn't know better, I would swear he's actually a teifling druid or something who was cursed because he cheesed off the wrong sorcerer. I promise, Ellie, I honestly think it's possible. Anyways, then he bolted into the house and ran straight in here. So, I did what anyone would do. I closed the door, right? I had no reason not to, especially since I thought you'd be coming inside relatively soon, and then we could work together to get him out of here before he could ruin anything. I was wrong, obviously, because then... Then! He hikes his front legs onto the stool and tries to eat one of my tarts. My tarts, Ellie. The ones I have meticulously perfected for the baking competition tomorrow!" She blows her nose on her apron and takes a shaky breath.

"I got so incredibly angry, Ellie. I couldn't see anything right, it was all red. I looked around for the first thing I could whack him with, which ended up being the broom, and tried to shoo him away from the hot pans so he couldn't knock them over. But did that work? No, no, it didn't. Not even in the slightest. Instead, he squealed and startled me. My hand knocked over an entire cup of melted butter, and I slipped, which threw me into the counter. I tried to catch myself, but couldn't before I knocked over the apple pie that had come out of the oven a moment before I went to open the door." I grab her hand and pat it gently, unsure of how to respond other than to let her continue her rant.

"That pie alone took me three hours because of the lattice work on the top. And then I'm in here trying to force him out, only for him to chase me instead. Then, I look up to see you standing there like some stupid statue while I struggle with that ignoramus, and now everything is ruined." Tears stream down her face again as she sobs, her shoulders shaking. "So many hours just down the drain. Or the pig trough, I guess. Because that's all this is good for now. I don't even know if I have time to remake even half of this before tomorrow. It's all just ruined."

My body stiffens, begging me to run as far away from the extraordinary emotional display as possible, and if I were with anyone else, I would have skulked away already. Instead, I wrap my arms around her as she continues to dissolve into a tear-leaking, snot-dripping, batter-covered mess. I force myself to stay strong, even when gagging when the custard and fruit filling soak through my trousers as the sticky crumbs and goo cover my feet.

I frequently shy away from anything involving emotional outbursts, not wanting to feel those emotions too deeply and express them incorrectly. Still, I can't ignore the tears burning my own eyes due to the sorrow that lies over us like a blanket as Kaida tries to regain her composure, only to lose it as soon as her breathing returns to normal.

Hoping it's the right thing and won't make her cry more, I awkwardly pull her into a hug and clear the clumps of damp green hair from her face. "What can Jareth and I do to be efficiently utilized so we can help you, Kai? I also want to tell you that I'm sorry. I didn't mean to freeze like a stupid statue when I came inside. I was just shocked, especially considering I had walked inside to tell you that he had vanished. Except he hadn't because I found him in here with you. I mean, honestly, try to see how it appeared from my end. My best friend, who loves animals more than anyone I have ever known, is in the kitchen chasing that porker around. Well, I guess he was actually chasing you, but that's beside the point. Either way you look at it, I came inside thinking the best possible thing had happened, instead of walking into that mess." Laughter builds in me as I recount my side of the story, and I try to stifle it. Despite my effort, I still chuckle.

"And then, Kai, I look up to see entire clouds of flour just poofing around." Another chuckle escapes, and Kaida's lip quirks. "And then there's you, who chased that stupid meathead with a broom handle, looking like a right warrior queen. I'll never look at you the same." I smile, and she returns it with a large, genuine smile of her own before laughter replaces the sobs that had just been wracking her body.

It takes us multiple attempts, but once we calm down, we help one another stand. My face speaks before I do, and Kaida laughs at my repulsion. "What's wrong, Ellie? The floor bothering you?"

I nod, scared to answer due to how close to puking I am. Thankfully, she unties her apron, folding it in half to cover the snotty bits, and lays in the floor for me to stand on. Hands on my hips, I inspect the room, surveying the extent of the damage caused by Tillard's chaos. As she does the same, tears threaten to well in Kaida's eyes again, and she shakes her head. "I honestly don't know if this is something that can be fixed, Ellie. He completely demolished hours, no days, of work. I put so much of myself into it, and I genuinely don't think we have the time to change that." Kaida's face flushes again.

I smile at her encouragingly. "Here's what we'll do. You go upstairs and take a bath. Get yourself cleaned up and soak in the tub until the tears and grumps are gone. I will stay down here and get all of this," I gesture around at the mess surrounding us, "cleaned up. When you get back, you'll return to a blank slate and a clean kitchen, and you can tell Jareth and me what you need us to do. We're here for you, Kai, however you need us to be. Now get your bum up there and get cleaned up, young lady. You're making me nauseous just staring at you."

With a pat to her back and a gentle shove, Kaida reluctantly leaves, and I try to locate the spot that will serve as my launching point. Broom in hand, I sweep the eggshells into the center of the room before grabbing the dishcloth out of the sink to scrape the crumbs from the island into the mess.

When Jareth walks in, he automatically makes his way to the sink to wash the dishes, even without asking where I need him. By the time Kaida returns, it's as if the unfortunate event from today never happened.

Beaming with my hands clasped tightly, I look at her. "Alright, Kai. Where do we start?"

The smile that blossoms across her face changes everything, and she looks at us before handing out orders. "I've never had an apprentice before, let alone two," she says after instructing Jareth to hand her the mixing bowls. "Eilaen, here is your list of what to do. Don't worry, you won't be doing any baking."

⌒⌒⌒⌒

When we break for dinner, we've already managed to replace half of the items, and Jareth and Kaida each have another batch ready to go. A meal of odds and ends in front of us, Kaida and I listen with glee as Jareth tells us tales from past festivals, keeping us entertained.

Animatedly, he recounts the story of the time Ms. Kestrel scared the other maze participants until she was the last gnome standing, ultimately winning the trophy. He slaps his knee with one hand, the other wiping the tear from his eye. "I've never seen anything like it. She's such a sweet lady, but she has a competitive streak wider than all of Smallburrow."

Next, he launches into a retelling of last year's festival, when the weather was a lot warmer than it normally is. Mayor Luddie, not wanting his citizens to risk overheating as they ran through the maze, decided at the last minute to host a fishing competition instead. Unsurprisingly, we learn the winners of that competition were none other than the elderly goblin couple who own Number Two Booth. They not only won the competition by a landslide, but also set a town record for the amount of fish they caught by using a traditional spear fishing method rather than modern fishing poles.

My favorite, however, ends up being the story of the year that a traveling clan of dwarves brought diamonds, emeralds, and loaded geodes, selling them by the sack from their traveling cart. Not a single soul left that year without something shiny in their hands.

The longer he retells his memories, the more I fall in love with this little town I've fallen in and, to our delight, he continues to wow us as we move back to our baking tasks. As the clock strikes midnight, we look around at the astronomical piles of pies, breads, cookies, and pastries. There's enough here to feed an army, and probably even then some!

It's evidence to prove we conquered the very feat Kaida had sworn today would be impossible, and there is a strange new sense of pride going through my heart and soul as I look upon our accomplishment.

As Kaida and I walk him to the door and bid Jareth goodnight, I'm overwhelmed with thankfulness and gratitude. Today had started with destruction and confusion, but somehow, the three of us could go to bed after achieving our goal of putting it all back together.

This, my heart whispers to me, *is my family*. One that I have actively helped create, rather than simply being pulled into and uncomfortably forced to pretend to be part of. It's one I've been able to find when I had nobody to call my own. I never thought it was possible to love and be loved by anyone in the same way I've experienced from Kaida, but I know without a shadow of a doubt I've quickly grown to feel the same way about our neighbors who embraced us just as wholly.

It's the same strange feeling I've been trying to place for the last few weeks, but have only now been able to.

This is the love of a true family.

The smile that spreads across my face as I lie in the

darkness of my room warms me, and as I slip off into a much-needed sleep, I'm more than certain it's the best feeling in the entire world.

The Autumn Festival

Despite the late hour at which I fell asleep, I'm awake before the sun and practically vibrating from my excitement. It's Autumn Festival Day! When I hear Kaida shuffling around her room, I get dressed and head downstairs to light the woodstove, ready to get the day started. After placing the kettle on the stovetop, I head out to do chores.

During the brisk walk, I repeat the affirmations I memorized as a youngster, determined not to allow myself to get in my own way. Today is going to be fun, and even though I don't perform my best when in social situations, I refuse to sabotage myself by going into it unprepared.

"I'm building lasting relationships, I want to succeed. I'm important to this town, and it's important to me. If stress gets me down, I don't need to worry. I'll just get somewhere quiet, even if I have to hurry."

The new rhyme comes to mind easily, and I turn it into a song, humming it as I work, quickly completing my chores, though I start with the chickens today. There's no way I'm going to risk Tillard wrecking things.

"You'd better be on your best behavior, Mister," I announce, cautiously opening the barn door. I stand in the doorway, hoping to prevent him from running out. To say I'm delighted when he stays stretched out in his pile of straw is an understatement, and he barely lifts his head to look at me as I close the door.

"He must be exhausted from yesterday," I whisper to the

cows as I place the stool between them.

I cannot believe how excited I am for the festival today, the nausea and anxiety that comes with knowing I'll be surrounded by noise and people at an all-time low. I laugh to myself, overjoyed at the development.

As I skip around the corner, I wave to Jareth and Ms. Kestrel, the two of them stepping through the gate to help Kaida and me pack and load the product of yesterday's work. We start with the heavier items, taking care not to put anything fragile or easily broken on the bottom. Carefully, I hitch Mable to the wagon and keep it as still as possible to keep Ms. Kestrel from falling as Jareth helps her onto the bench.

As soon as Kaida and I get in, I grab the reins, and we head off to town. When we arrive at the festival grounds, Jareth and I quickly unload everything, while Ms. Kestrel leads Kaida to the table to get registered for the big competition. When we're done, Jareth and I run to meet our friends, arriving just as Kaida personally hands Urzal her entry pie.

Anxiety takes control, Kaida shoos Jareth and me away so she can organize and price the remaining items that she brought for the bake sale. "You two enjoy yourselves," Kaida cries out, her hands already busy moving things around and putting the pricing plaques out.

"Come on," I tell Jareth as I link my arm through his. "It'll be my turn to stand watch soon, and I don't want to miss anything."

We take our time going through the merchant booths, *oohing* and *ahhing* at the unique items everyone has. When we reach the end, Jareth looks around forlornly. "Ah, man. I was hoping the dwarves were going to be here this year. I wanted another gem to add to my collection."

As we bob and weave through the other areas, we greet everyone, though it doesn't take us long before we run out of people to exchange pleasantries with. The more we walk, the more my heart threatens to burst from my chest with all of the pride I've become familiar with. Everyone put their entire beings into making this the best Autumn Festival to date, and even with it being my first one, I'd be lying if I were to say that I'm fairly certain we have accomplished that goal.

The scents of pumpkin, caramel, and cinnamon spice fill every nook and cranny possible. It pairs perfectly with the syrupy-sweetness in the air from the apple cider Urzal's great-uncle is serving in the middle of Town Square. It doesn't take much begging to convince me to try it, and the drink bathes my insides with its autumnal warmth.

Several tables are covered with ghosties and bats; others are loaded with candy and sugary sweets. My favorite one, though, has to be the table with tiny trinkets depicting comedically exaggerated goblins and ghouls.

There is not a single standing structure that's been left untouched by the decorating community, and their dedication and hard work speak to their attention to detail and desire for perfection. It even appears as if the trees wanted to get in on the festival spirit and have changed colors in the last week. The swirling leaves of browns, yellows, and reds float through the air as the wind strips them from their former home, blowing them around everyone.

Lost in my head, it takes a few steps for me to realize that Jareth is no longer at my side, and I turn my head to find him two tables behind me. Confused, I call his name. "What are you doing?" I ask, turning around and joining him again.

"Eilaen, I- I wanted to talk to you about something. About the kiss on your birthday. I-," he stammers. Not wanting to rehash the incident, I interrupt him before he can get any further.

"Oh. Yes. That. I, uh, kind of thought we were going to, ya know, pretend like it didn't happen. Isn't that what we've been doing anyway?" I twist my hands together and smile at him with uncertainty.

He inhales deeply, puffing it out in a hard breath. "See, I thought about that, and I've tried being okay with leaving it where it's been. But, I can't. I want to explain myself. Get it all out on the table so we can officially put it behind us without any loose threads. I like you, Eilaen. You're amazingly talented, and I have never met anyone else who was able to hone in on their magic as quickly as you." He moves his arm behind him and rubs the back of his neck anxiously.

"You make me laugh, and I really enjoy spending time with you. The, uh, you know, made me really reflect on my actions and how I really feel about you. It honestly relieved me to realize that I only care for you as a friend. Well, more like family. But you know what I mean." His words are spoken gently, almost as if he's trying not to hurt my feelings, which makes me want to laugh.

So I do. The air around us loses the tension in it at his confession. "Oh, thank goodness! That's so good to know. I mean, don't get me wrong. I'm sure you're probably not a bad person to kiss, and you are kind of handsome. But I have never felt anything for you romantically. At all. You're like a pesky brother, and you've quickly grown on me like a fungus on a log. I'm glad I can consider you to be part of my family, Jareth."

Tension melts from his shoulders visibly as they relax into a slouch. "Well, now that we've gotten that sorted out, we've gotta get back to Kaida. I'm starving, and there are a couple of pumpkin and cream cheese tarts with my name all over them." He claps his hands and rubs them together before his arm loops through mine again.

We awkwardly and lopsidedly skip back to Number One Book. Upon our arrival, we see an astonished Kaida behind the table. "I've sold out of almost everything!" she exclaims, her hands pressing against her cheeks.

The child-like joy covering her face could melt even the coldest heart, and Ms. Kestrel sits next to her, deep in thought, as she finishes counting the coins made today. In one hand, she holds a wooden writing utensil, with her free hand holding down the piece of parchment with numbers scribbled on it.

"Kaida, dear. If my calculations are correct, and we all know they are seldom wrong, you've made your largest profit yet." The elderly gnome looks at Kaida as if she were her own grandchild held in high regard.

Kaida's window-shattering squeal forces me to cover my ears and hope my eardrums have shattered. Leaning over to see for myself, my jaw drops, and my eyes dart to Kaida's.

"Kaida, you did it!" I yell as she screams, "I'm getting my bakery," loud enough for all to hear. Our excitement draws a crowd, the attendees all clapping and cheering with us.

"You can open a bakery! We can get rid of Tillard! You can do whatever you want to do!" I exclaim, wrapping my hands around her wrists as we jump in excitement.

Jareth wraps his arms around us, effectively stopping us from jumping, and congratulates her. "To think you could have had more if it wasn't for Tillard. Nah, what am I saying? It was definitely because of my help."

When Kaida wriggles away from him and swats at him, he takes a large step out of her reach and antagonises her with a silly face.

"Would you like some help finding a storefront, Kaida, or do you already have one in mind?" Ms. Kestrel asks, still smiling.

For the second time in as many days, I look upon my family, filled to the brim with love and admiration. My heart overflows with joy and happiness in an amount I'll never be able to adequately quantify. Not even the chill in the air can bring me down, the emotional outpour warming me more than any fire or cuppa has ever done, and probably never will.

"Will all of our bakers participating in today's competition please line up at the judging table so we can begin?" Mayor Luddie's voice booms over the crowd.

Kaida looks at me, eyes wide with anticipation, and she gives us a small wave before skipping off to the town's entrance into the market, where the table is set up. Beside it is a second table, this one with four chairs lined up behind it. In each seat is a judge. Between the tables is the podium, where Mayor Luddie stands as the contestants file to the front.

Jareth, Ms. Kestrel, and I make our way to the front of the crowd, standing in the front row. On the surface, Kaida looks calm and unnerved unless you know her tell-tale signs of anxiety eating away at her. I look, and there it is, her two most common that she's so anxious she can barely breathe; she's biting the corner of her lip while one hand picks at the nail bed of the other.

As the judges deliberate, a cloud of nervous energy hangs over the crowd, and collectively, we hold our breath. Within moments, Mayor Luddie stands, straightening his tie andjacket as he steps on the podium once more. After clearing his throat to gain our attention, his voice echoes through the space again. "Residents of Smallburrow, if I may have your attention again. I'd like to start by taking a moment to thank you all for attending the annual Autumn Festival. As we had hoped, this year has been the best so far, and it's all thanks to all who helped put it together. I couldn't be prouder of you all or ask for a better town to be part of. So, thank you, Smallburrow, for loving our home the way you do." He pauses, and the building anticipation is almost thick enough to cut.

"It's no secret that our small town has been thoroughly enamored by the arrival of Eilaen and Kaida. For those who may be unaware, these two bright halflings picked up everything to move to our town so they could take ownership of Mapleground Farm following the passing of our dear friend, Jakoby Mapleground, may he rest in peace. Together, they have not only brought a much-needed joy back to our community, but they've also had several of us loosening our waistbands from the delectable pastries Kaida brings to the market each week."The crowd chuckles at his sentiment, and Ms. Kestrel grasps my hand tenderly.

He unfolds the paper in his hand. "It's not every year that a newcomer comes in and brings the panel to a unanimous decision, nor is it every year that ole Mr. Finkle's rhubarb pie is knocked out of first place. However, it's my pleasure to announce that, yes, Kaida. It seems as if one can bake her cake and eat it, too. Congratulations, Kaida Leavensen. You have won first place with your apple spice tartlettes! If you wouldn't mind coming over and accepting your blue ribbon, this certificate is good for two free months of booth space for Number One Booth, and the coin prize allotting to 100 gold coins." Graciously, Kaida accepts her prizes and gives the mayor a hug before turning towards her clapping audience.

"Thank you, everyone! What an honor. Don't forget to stop by Number One Booth next week for all your pastry needs," she says loudly.

Though we're a stone's throw away, the mass of townsfolk that surrounds her prevents her from getting to us. Once she's free, she bolts towards us, laughing and carefree. With broad smiles and open arms, we welcome her and wrap her in our collective embrace, snacking on the remaining treats as we wait for the maze gate to open.

What a Maze!

The afternoon soon fades into night, the sky shifting from sunny to dark blue and starry.

The crickets play their nightly song, their tune tonight immediately followed by the bell that signals the maze is about to open. The energy now surrounding the festival is frenzied as we all move towards maze's gate, which is being closely guarded by an orc who looks like he could be related to the mayor.

Nerves wiggle in my stomach, but there's no time for me to find somewhere quiet to hide. Anxiety buzzes under my skin, electrifying my senses uncomfortably. I bounce on the soles of my feet, hoping the steady movement will release some of the tension building in me.

"Are you okay?" Kaida whispers, giving my hand a tight squeeze.

I give her a small nod, and she smiles reassuringly. A heartbeat later, Mayor Luddie blows on a whistle, the shrill noise setting me further on the edge of becoming an overstimulated basket case. The sound of a popping toy echoes around us, and just like that, it's go time, and the race for the Great Golden Pumpkin is on!

The ensuing chaos is maddening as everyone around us pushes their way through the single-person gate before scattering in every direction imaginable.

Kaida doesn't let go of my hand and, together, we stumble

around the maze for what feels like forever. At one point, Kaida and I hold our breaths as we get the show of a lifetime while watching Ms. Kestrel's small form sneaks up behind a goblin and startles him, his cries of surprise morphing hilariously into a rapid string of curses. We scarcely hold in our laughter until they're both out of sight, but once neither is visible, Kaida and I fall to the ground in hysterics as we clutch our middles.

A few turns later, we watch in horror as a female orc stumbles headfirst over an unseen sprite who had been hiding in the roughage. The poor thing is so scared, it shoots up into the air, yelping about almost dying.

After one too many wrong turns and dead ends, weariness settles over me. *Are we ever going to make it to the center?* Probably not at this rate.

Kaida whines. "If we get lost and die in here, I hope someone tells Tillard how successful I was today, despite his antics."

"Maybe we'll accidentally turn ourselves around and wander through the exit," I suggest, though I know it's not likely.

Surely we've gone further inside this maze than that? Everything looks the same, though, so it's too hard to tell the beginning from the ending. Maybe I'm just not cut out for mazes. Too much unknown, and I just want to go to bed.

We stumble through another archway, and as we try to make a decision on which direction to turn, a loud, victorious cry comes from somewhere in front of us. Though barely audible, it's obvious that it's the Golden Pumpkin winner as they celebrate.

Suddenly, a shadowed figure plows through the bushes, knocking me onto my bum. With a startled cry, I look up to see that my attacker is none other than Jareth.

"Oh, thank goodness. It's just you," I say, letting out a breath of relief and taking the hand he extends to me.

"Eilaen! I am so sorry! I didn't see you. It's so dark, and you're not, erm, very tall. Honestly, I'm glad I didn't knock Kaida over, too. Are you looking for the way out?" He struggles to speak while catching his breath, pretending not to see my offense at being called out for my lack of height. Then, he places one hand on my shoulder and the other on Kaida's and turns us around.

"C'mon. This way you two."

"Who won?" Kaida asks as we follow behind him.

He doesn't turn around as he replies animatedly, his hands flying in the air. "You two will never believe it! It was incredible. Never in my wildest dreams did I think I would see a pixie win the maze challenge. And for it to be such a teeny one, at that!"

"We need a little more information, Jar," I remind him, to which he smacks his hand—I think it's his hand, anyway—against his forehead in reply.

"Okay. It's one of the new pixies from the family that lives next to Nadles. You know, the cute little one who keeps trying to catch the fish over in the forest lake? She just so happened to stumble onto it. Literally just tripped and landed next to the pumpkin. If I hadn't witnessed it, I wouldn't believe it really happened. I mean, a teeny pixie? Really?" He shakes his head before looking at us as Kaida stumbles toward the right.

"Ah, not that way, Kai. This way." We turn to the left. "Something to remember in case Urzal hires these guys to do the maze for next year: they don't use what most consider to be typical maze construction materials. It's all enchanted, which means you can't walk with your hands against the wall. It's designed so anyone who does so will get lost."

"Now that you mention it, it does seem to be taking less time on our way out than it did for us to get however far we got," Kaida muses.

Finally, we come up to the gate, and the three of us release a weary breath at the knowledge that the end is near.

"You know what, Jareth? I'm not even upset that you ran into me now." I look around, not seeing our last party member. "Do we need to stand here and wait for Ms. Kestrel or start loading our things up?

"Let's load it all up. If we're not here when she comes out, she'll meet us at the wagon," Jareth replies, and we trudge through our exhaustion to Number One Booth.

Urzal and Ms. Kestrel both appear at Mabel's side just as Jareth tosses the final basket into the back of the wagon, the two of them whispering conspiratorially.

A thick blanket of exhaustion weighs over us as we moan

and groan, climbing into the wagon so we can head home. My body is tired and achy, and my bones are even exhausted from everything today has contained.

We're almost home when Kaida lets out the loudest yawn of her life and then slumps over to drop her head onto my shoulder. With a sleepy sigh, she nudges her body gently into my side. "Ellie, I think this adventure has been the grandest one we could have ever taken. I'm so glad we have been able to travel through it together."

I rest my cheek against the top of her head, unable to stop a smile from forming. "Me too, Kai. Thanks for convincing me that it would be worth it," I chuckle. "Who would have thought that a letter that caused me such anxiety over the summer was going to bring us to the life we're living now?"

We complete our ride in silence, other than some light snoring from Jareth, and contentment brushes over me as if it were a breeze on a warm spring day. Not only have I made this experience in Smallburrow something enjoyable, but I've also been able to make the farm a place I can be proud of. Still, even that doesn't compare to what brings me more joy than I've known in all of my existence. I

In taking this chance, I've found so much love, support, and family in Jareth and Ms. Kestrel. More than should be possible for one person to hold within their hearts. We might make quite the motley crew, but there is nobody else that I want to go through this life with.

As I encourage a sleepy Mabel to continue trotting home, another thought comes to me, sustaining me with just enough energy to finish the ride without falling asleep. *Maybe adventure is less about the length of the journey we travel and more about the people we meet along the way.*

Driving the wagon through the farm gates, I'm more certain of the new me than I've ever been. Whatever happens from this moment on, I'm not the same halfling I had been when we crossed the threshold of Mapleground Farm, and I know all of the credit belongs to the three beings who choose to accept me as I am every day.

The Magic of Winter

Icy air hits my foot as it pokes out of my blanket. I crack my eyes open, groaning when I see the sun is barely rising. My arms are like weights attached to my shoulders. I knew there would be repercussions today, but I wasn't expecting those to be exhaustion wrapping itself around my body. Raising slowly, my stiff joints pop and, when the blanket drops off of me, the cold grips me tightly.

I yelp, scrambling across the room so that I can bury myself in my warmest robe and pair of thick stockings, and though I'm warmer in them, it's still not enough. I tiptoe down the stairs, vigorously rubbing my arms, unnerved by the white clouds forming with every breath.

I need my work boots.

After jamming my feet into my boots, which I'm thankful provide instant warmth to my lower digits, I hustle to the fireplace. Need to ask Jareth if he can get us more brought inside later, I tell myself as I toss in the last two logs in the stack, hoping I won't forget. With kindling on top, I light a match and toss it in, blowing the flame across the paper scraps to help it spread.

The logs catch quicker than I anticipate, the warmth licking its way through the layers of my skin as it seeps into my bones. I reach my hands out, groaning in relief when my fingers thaw, and I wriggle them to help bring the sensation back into them.

No longer in danger of being a halfling popsicle, I shuffle

into the kitchen and light the wood stove, noting that its wood storage also needs replenishing. That can wait a little while, I remind myself as I fill the kettle and set out everything I need to make myself a cup of tea. The white puffs are thicker in the kitchen without the warmth of the large fireplace here to counter the cold, and as I wait for the kettle to sing, I return to my room and dress for the weather.

The thick woolen tunic I grab reminds me of summer leaves, and paired with my favorite grey trousers, I almost feel put together for once. I go to leave my room, but stop in the doorway when I remember my winter cloak in my bottom drawer.

With it around my shoulders, I melt beneath its fabric, and I'm finally comfortable to brave the outdoors. As I pass her closed door, Kaida calls my name. "Please tell me the fire is going downstairs because I am frozen!"

"Yes," I reply, thankful my teeth are no longer clacking together, even if it's only for now. "Fireplace is blazing, stove is on, and the kettle should be ready soon. Can you handle the tea while I go check on the animals?"

"As long as it's nice and toasty downstairs, I'll do anything you ask. I think my toes are about to fall off from being so cold."

I chuckle and talk myself into braving the outdoors, glad there will be a warm drink waiting inside when I return. The blast of air I meet when the door opens slices through the exposed skin on my face, and I gasp. As quickly as I can, I traipse through the tall, crunchy grass in the field, arriving at the barn breathless.

"Tillard better not try anything today," I mutter under my breath. "If he wants to turn into a pigscicle, I'll let him."

It's taking more effort than I care to admit, between the cold and exhaustion, and if it weren't because the animals need me, I would still be inside where it's cozy.

Winter has definitely arrived, and it's rearing its ugly head far too soon for my tastes. Ha. Happy winter, indeed.

Once behind the barn door, I sprint to the wood stove, lighting it before grabbing the pitchfork and tossing the hay out in four equal bundles. This time, I don't bother attempting to milk the cows. They've been giving less and less each day this week, and I have learned enough to know whatever drops I get today won't be sufficient to use. Behind me, the noises of gratitude from the animals fill the raggedy red building, and I look back to see all five—Tillard included—huddled by the stove.

I cup my hands in front of me, blowing as hard as I can to keep them warm as I move from the barn to the stable. My nose is so cold that as soon as my hands move to my side, the ache from it thawing radiates across the center of my face.

Desperatel to finish, I rush through feeding Mabel and her stall mate, Sorrel, the donkey Kaida has named and give them each an extra bale of hay to keep them warm. Before heading out, I hover by their stove, trying to soak in as much of the heat as I can. The chickens are never thrilled when I intrude on their coop, and they make sure I know it. I don't want to risk their wrath just to stand in front of their stove for a moment or two.

Before I head back into the house, I look across the yard and soak in the beauty of it all. The sun glimmers across the frost-covered grass. Even as I rub my arms hard enough that it almost knocks me over, I still can't believe this chunk of peace belongs to me.

That is, until my eyes reach the garden. Not a single plot has been left untouched, the cold having withered it to nothing during the night. It's all dead—every stalk, every sprout, every branch. Everything is brown and brittle.

Despite the cold, I stop in front of it and drop to my knees, the frozen ground brutal and callous under me. The dampness of tears rolling down my cheeks can't even compare to the brokenness of my heart as the truth sinks in.

There's no coming back from this. Not now, not even if I run as fast as my stocky legs will carry me to Jareth. There's simply no way this can be reversed. Though the signs had pointed to the cold coming in, the sweeping in overnight caught me off guard. Our lack of preparation has left us vulnerable, and now I see what that looks like. I hadn't expected it to sweep in overnight, and our lack of preparation has left us vulnerable.

An overwhelming sadness covers me, its weight on my chest making it hard for me to breathe. My own kitchen has nothing in it for the winter, nor have I been able to gather enough for the entirety of Smallburrow. The emptiness that rides on sorrow's coattails adds more weight to me, and my tears continue to flow. Hopelessness squeezes my lungs; its grasp is harsh and unforgiving.

There are a small handful of plots that have the potential for reviving, though I honestly don't believe my magic will be enough to do it. I lean over, clutching my sides as despair further wraps around me. My thoughts beat at me, telling me that this is all my fault, that there's no way I can do this, that my magic will never be enough to handle something of this magnitude.

"I haven't even had the chance to grow it enough to try," I whisper, the wind deafening my words.

Sniffling, I wipe the salty drops from my face before using the corner of my cloak to wipe the half-frozen drips away from my nose. Heartbroken isn't a strong enough word to describe my state of being, but I still attempt to stir up the dredges of determination I still have.

If I cannot do this on my own, I'll get Jareth to tell me how much we can save. Maybe he can also help fill in whatever gaps remain afterwards.

Starting with the herbs, I stand with my eyes closed and palms facing down, begging my magic to spark. When that doesn't work, I take a breath and try again. This time, I call it forward, willing it to flow from my hands and to heal everything in front of me. Then I recall some of my happiest memories, remembering what Jareth had told us about being intentional with our magic.

I think about eating Kaida's raspberry lemon tarts in the summer and the way sandy beaches feel between my toes. Then I remember how it felt when I first summoned my magic, and the intense joy it gave me. Finally, I think about last night when I watched Kaida being presented with her prizes and celebrating with her and our neighbors, our family.

The most recent memory fades, and in its place, the lingering warmth slips through me before settling in my hands. The bright, yellow light flows from them once again, almost blinding me as I open my eyes. I lower them, dimming the light until it resembles the evening's sunrays, ecstatic at the thriving herbs I find under them.

I move from the herbs to the plots with the produce most likely to have survived, hoping it wouldn't require as much of me as the rest. From there, I go plot to plot, my newfound hope sustaining me as the overwhelming despair dissipates.

Row by row, I travel slowly through the garden until I have thoroughly exhausted myself, disappointment flaring when I see I still have more than halfway to go.

"I cannot do this," I cry, plopping onto the ground wearily.

My mistake is instantly apparent when I try to stand, my legs shakily supporting me, but only just barely. By the time I pull myself across the threshold of the house, I'm practically crawling at a snail's pace. Somehow, I finally make it to the den, getting onto the sofa before almost passing out.

I don't hear or see Kaida enter the room, but I hear the drowning echo of her yelp as she sees the state I've returned in. My eyes flutter shut, unable to stay open. My mind is shrouded in a thick fog as I dissociate from the real world. Maybe I'll feel better after I take a nap.

⌁⌁⌁

In my exhaustion-induced haze, I hear the distorted sounds of people talking, but I'm uncertain of who it is or how long I've been suspended in the hibernation-like state I can't seem to force myself out of.

One of the voices echoes distortedly when someone gives an explanation that makes sense, even to me. "One of the side effects of magic is that it can drain you of your strength if you push yourself too far when using it, and I think that's what happened to Eilaen. All we can do is wait until her body regains enough stamina and she wakes up."

Bright lights blind me when I blink awake. I don't know what time it is or what day it is. I rapidly blink, trying to see what's going on around me, but when my vision clears, I'm looking at the ceiling. Reluctantly, I pull myself up to rest on my elbows, but whenever I try to move any further, I drop down. My chest heaves from the exertion, and it's almost as if someone has replaced every single bone in me with iridium bars while I slept.

"Ellie!" Kaida's voice comes from my left, and her footsteps patter across the floor. Her warm skin touches mine, and her sparkling eyes are full of concern when they meet mine. "You're finally awake. Are you okay? Can I get you anything?"

I cough, realizing how dry my throat is. "Can I get a hot cup of tea?" I ask slowly, my voice raspy even though I'm swallowing what little saliva I have after every other word.

She bounces to her feet and rushes out of the room, coming back fairly quickly with a cup of butterscotch tea in one hand and a slice of pecan pie in the other.

"For your strength," she explains, gently placing them on the table next to my bed. Wrapping her arms around me, she helps me sit up and puts an extra pillow behind me to keep me propped up.

The cup shakes in my hand; it's too much for me to handle on my own. I grunt in exasperation when Kaida takes it from me and not only brings it to my mouth for me to drink, but also feeds me.

"How long?" I ask after swallowing my last bite. I already feel stronger, and my arms are less like the heavy metal bars and more like normal weights; still harder to move than usual, but we're on the right track.

Before she can answer, Jareth knocks on the door and enters. "Oh, good, you're awake. I was hoping it wouldn't be too much longer." His cheery voice, for once, is a breath of fresh air, and I smile weakly. "Do you remember anything from when you passed out?" he asks, pulling over a stool and sitting by the bed.

"It was cold, and I went to do my normal chores. It was okay until I got to the garden and-," I jump up, ignoring my spinning head and the ringing in my ears. "The garden! Is it alright? Did it all die?" Tears well in my eyes at the idea that all of my work had been for nothing because I allowed myself to do too much without help.

"It's all okay. I walked through the door not too long after your collapse. That was three days ago. You should have come to me for help, El. A job that large is too much for anyone to do alone, especially one who hasn't had a chance to grow their magical stores."

"You scared us, Ellie," Kaida says, still at my side. Her voice is small, so unlike her typical fiestiness, and guilt flares to life inside me.

"You're right, and I am so sorry. I should have asked for help or even just waited for you to come check things out. It was just so hard to see everything dead or dying, and I needed to do something so that I wouldn't fall apart because of it. Not my best idea, though, from the looks of it." I lean back, hoping it'll ease some of the discomfort in my head.

"If it makes you feel any better, though, I feel like I got into a fight with Tillard and lost." My weak attempt at a joke draws out a chuckle from each of my friends, though it only leaves me breathless. I wince as I attempt to reposition myself, my muscles screaming at me for doing so.

Jareth stands, his hands on his hips. He twists his lips to the side, deep in concentration. "Kaida, do you think you can help me get Eilaen downstairs and to the garden? I want to show her something."

"Absolutely," she replies. "Give me a second, though. I'll be right back."

She leaves, and the stairs creak as she steps down them, leaving me to wonder what these two are cooking up. When she returns, her triumphant smile is unnerving. "Okay. Ready."

"Where are we going? Hello?" I ask, only to be met with silence.

Instead of answering my questions or protests to stay put, the two of them work to assist me down the stairs and into the garden. As they lower me to the stool Kaida demands I use, I look around in wonder. *How is everything so green and bright?*

The scene before me gobsmacks me, and I whip my head to look at Jareth. "What.. What did you do, Jareth? How did you do all of this?" I ask.

I want to learn how to make a garden flourish so beautifully, like he's apparently done since I've been asleep.

"I didn't do this," he answers, stretching his arms widely on either side. "You did all of this."

My jaw drops so quickly that I have a momentary flash of

concern that I may have injured myself again. When I was out here last, so much of this garden had been gray and dead. But now? It's as if the freeze never happened. Everything around me is in full bloom as if by magic.

My magic.

Giddiness takes over as I hobble to my feet and lurch forward, unable to comprehend what I'm seeing. Everything from flower beds in the front to the herb plots under the window to the dormant fruit trees... It's all thriving, and even the newer plants are heavy with produce.

Nothing has been left untouched by the magic that can only come from nurturing, from someone who truly cares.

"Oh, my goodness me. It- it's beautiful," Kaida whispers, her face full of wonder. "Your dream, Ellie. Your dream. It's finally in your hands." Her eyes shine with unshed tears, and though I try to blink them away, they pool in my own as well.

As her words sink in, no amount of willpower or blinking works, and the tears stream from my eyes and down my cheeks. She's right. *This* is the start of my dream—the actual start of it. Something happened that day, and though I may never know what it truly was, it helped me to use my magic in a way that I'll be able to provide for our town for the entire season, if not longer.

It's everything I have ever wanted it to be, and yet, it's so much more. This dream I've been holding in my heart for so long is coming true. Not even wishing on a star could have made it happen quite like this. The happiness that fills my heart grants me an immeasurable amount of strength, and with it comes the knowledge that I'm capable of doing this, the latter hitting me in the chest before spreading through me like a warm embrace.

Maybe everyone in town is right. Maybe Smallburrow truly is, in itself, magical.

I gasp as a sudden idea comes to mind and look at the two friends with me. "We need to get Ms. Kestrel here. I think I'm going to need all three of you for this."

Buried in Friendship (...and Produce)

Jareth runs to get Ms. Kestrel while Kaida and I set up everything we need for the meeting I've called. If this plan is going to work, I'll need every ounce of help I can get. Once we're all around the table, I stand with my palms firmly pressing into the cool wood.

"Tomorrow is the last market day of the season, and we all know how badly I want to get as much produce to the residents as I can. Ms. Kestrel, do you know anyone with magic that can enchant a box with ice on the inside so the contents stay cold over a long period of time? I need the produce to stay fresh until the weather is cold enough to leave items outside for longer periods of time."

Rubbing her chin with her hand, the elderly gnome contemplates for a beat before her face lights up. "I believe so, girlie. Let me call on some of my old friends to see if they or anyone they know can help. It might take a day or two to hear back, though."

I nod before turning toward Kaida and Jareth. "I hope you two are ready to put your muscles to work, because I need the extra hands to get everything out there harvested. Then we'll need to sort it into categories. I won't lie. This job is going to require a lot of work mentally, too."

The two of them nod, and as Jareth rolls his sleeves up to his elbows, he gives me a crooked thumbs-up. "Let's do it! The sun will be setting soon, and the nights are bitterly cold already. The sooner we get out there, the sooner we can be done," he says, standing.

Walking with us to the door, Ms. Kestrel takes my elbow. "I will handle getting a hot supper cooked for you three. You're going to want something hearty to warm your bellies by the time you finish."

Running around the house, Kaida and I gather all of the wicker baskets we can find and meet Jareth at the garden, where he's already elbow deep in his first plot. As we work, we settle into a rhythm: Jareth takes care of the plants that are too tall for Kaida and me, while the two of us are in charge of gathering everything close to the ground. We, then, tackle things like carrots, potatoes, onions, and garlic together, the smaller roots and stalks taking extra time to pluck from the frozen ground.

As predicted, it doesn't take long for the sky to darken and the air to take on a noticeable bite. Still, I refuse to let the weariness slow me down and, with a firm resolve settling over me, I push forward.

There's just too much to do, I remind myself as I trudge forward, refusing to quit.

We've barely touched half of it when we collapse in a heap of arms and legs. When I realize they're both huffing and heaving, I don't feel nearly as down about how badly out of breath I was a moment ago, which is nice to experience for once.

Kaida whines as her head swivels around. "You guys, we're almost out of space in the wagon and the house. I'm beginning to think that maybe there's a reason why farms aren't usually in full bloom year-round."

Jareth and I make small noises in agreement, but I'm left with the conundrum of where to store it all. This is Plan A, and there is no Plan B. "Come on. Let's go inside and warm up while we figure out where to go from here." I grab the closest two baskets and stand, using what's left of my energy to carry them into the house while avoiding the produce scattered all over the floor.

Wracked with exhaustion, we make the hard decision to sit at the table. With resignation, I know better than to get cozy in the den if I want to get anything else done. Getting comfortable on the sofa or in a chair will do nothing but sap the remainder of my determination, and judging by the looks on their faces, Kaida and Jareth have come to the same conclusions.

My bum barely has a chance to connect with the seat when Ms. Kestrel whips around the table with four bowls, one at each seat. Silently, she returns to the kitchen long enough to grab a tray carrying four mugs and insists on caring for us while we rest. When she's seated, we dig in, and I inhale my food so quickly that I can't register any of the flavors in it. Still hungry, I scurry to refill my bowl and savor the warmth and flavors it holds.

Jareth is the first one finished, standing before leaning to his left and wrapping his arms around our adopted grandmother. Kaida and I scramble to get next to them, joining the embrace.

"You youngins are sweet, and I hate to end such a loving gesture. But Jareth, you stink, and I need you to let go of me so I'm no longer subjected to the odor wafting from under your arms." Her voice is muffled and, with a laugh, we all release her and return to our seats.

The room grows quiet once more, and I wish I could peer into the minds of everyone as we try to figure out how to make my idea work.

Kaida's the first to speak, her words coming out slow and uncertain. "I suppose we could, maybe, ask the townspeople for help."

Why didn't I think of that?

"Kai. That might be the most brilliant idea that you have had all week," I reply enthusiastically, shooting to my feet. "I was wanting to surprise Smallburrow with all of it, but that idea sounds ridiculous now that I'm voicing it. Besides, if we can get the entire town to help, we won't have to do it all in one night."

"Plus, it's cold enough that whatever is left out there tonight should be okay for a day or two," Jareth says, chiming in.

Excitedly, we chatter as our food settles, quickly realizing our biggest hurdle will be getting the townsfolk to the farm to collect their produce, rather than us taking it to the market and selling it.

As long as Jareth and I can keep everything alive the entire season, there is no real reason why this can't work. Together, we agree that this plan is officially our new Plan A, and we're choosing to forgo forming a Plan B altogether.

Energetically, Kaida dances into the kitchen, the familiar sounds of her baking filling the space. "Decision making," she states loudly, "always makes me need something sweet."

Before long, the mouthwatering scents of chocolate, butter, and cinnamon mingle, wafting in from the kitchen, and we wait in anticipation for Kaida to bring her latest concoction out for us to try.

"Okay, you guys. Try this," she says, carrying out a tray of treats.

She stuffs a large hunk of something into my mouth so quickly I don't have time to process it, much less stop her. Yet all it takes is that one bite of whatever it is to make me okay with her startling lack of impulse control.

It's light and flaky, with the slightest hints of butter and cinnamon sugar swirling in my mouth. I immediately ask for another, delighting myself in it. The warm, melty goodness of the chocolate inside is so intense I can't stop myself from groaning aloud.

"I don't know what you've made this time, Kai. But I think it might be the most incredible thing you've ever made." I grab another from the platter and pop it into my mouth.

Her eyes twinkle in amusement at my reaction. "If you think that's great, wait until you try it with a mug of hot cocoa!"

Jareth's sleepy body quickly perks as the platter appears in front of him. "I will never know what I have done to deserve these delectable pieces of art whenever I step foot into this house." The muffled words are scarcely understandable as he speaks around his mouthful of food, but his delight is as clear as glass.

"I always make my friends the very best of my treats. So if you're eating that good here, I guess that would make you one of my very best of friends," Kaida replies, poking him between two of his ribs and causing him to flinch.

"Oh dear. What does that mean for a little ole gnome like me?" Ms. Kestrel jokes, snatching a pastry from Jareth's hand, the gesture eliciting a giggle from Kaida at his expression.

"It means I love you the most. Other than Eilaen, that is," she replies sweetly, plucking the last pastry off the platter before Jareth can reach it and stuffing it into her mouth to keep it from getting taken.

Looking from Kaida to Jareth, then to Ms. Kestrel, I am overcome with gratitude for being pulled into this family. *We may all be different, and none of us looks like the others. In the ways that matter, though, we're the same.* It's a realization that makes my heart swell with every ounce of love I possess.

The next morning, as I drift from the barn after tending the animals, I wave to Ms. Kestrel as she strides down the path towards the door. "Good morning!"

She waves back, her smile stretching across her face so wide that it crinkles the thin, dark skin at the corner of her eyes. "Good morning, girlie. Nice to see you out with the chickens this morning. She wraps me in her warm embrace, shivering when her cloak slips off her shoulder.

"Let's get inside. It's a wee bit nipply out here this morning," I suggest, motioning for her to go in before me.

Once inside, I take her cloak and place it on a low-hanging hook beside the door, and we quickly shuffle to the den where Kaida, bless her soul, is standing in front of the fire with two steaming mugs and a platter of cinnamon apple turnovers.

"I heard you two outside and thought you'd like something to warm up with before it's time to leave." Her cheerful voice fills the room with love in a way only she can.

Ms. Kestrel grabs a turnover and a mug before moving to sit in the low-seated chair closest to the fireplace. "Eilaen, I thought you'd like to know that after I went home last night, I reached out to some folks in search of your magic ice box." Her words come out fast, coated in excitement. "I haven't found anyone specifically, but I am pleased to say that your idea has been well-received by those I spoke to and has also spurred some of our townsfolk into action." She pauses to take a sip of her tea, clearing her throat as she sets it on the table beside her.

"There is a high elf who owns a shop downtown who told me he knows a wizard who can create the icebox you're needing. It'll be here the day after tomorrow, which should give your plans time to spread. I suspect your plan will catch on like fire once it makes its rounds. Hopefully, that will also give you the time you need to get everything together without forcing you to overreach. Again." The pointed stare she gives me is enough to remind me of what that looks like.

Forgetting the mug in my hand, I jump and almost spill it, leaping across the room to hug her. "Ms. Kestrel, you are truly one of life's biggest blessings. I hope you know how thankful I am for you."

When Jareth arrives, we transfer Kaida's baked goods, as well as the more fragile produce, to the wagon. For the first time since I've been here, it's filled to the brim, amazing me at how much it's able to hold.

"Hopefully we don't have to reload most of this at the end of the day," I whisper to Kaida, who startles at the idea of bringing it home.

Ms. Kestrel speaks, grabbing my attention as she thanks Jareth for helping her into the wagon. "Thank you, boy. I'm an old gnome, dontcha know? Sometimes, I even forget until these bones remind me." She pinches one of his cheeks, wincing when she shakes her arm around, rubbing her elbow as she lowers it.

I give the house one last check before locking it for the day. As I slip the key into my pocket, a squeal rings out. Not just any squeal, either, but one that has only been uttered by one single, specific pig that lives on this farm.

Tillard.

I have enough time to whip my head around before I find him barrelling towards me. Unlike his most recent attempts to knock me down, he's too close for me to jump out of the way before his massive head crashes into my knees. I'm instantly knocked to the ground, hearing the cries of Jareth and Kaida as they run to help.

Together, they help me to my feet, standing me in a way that I'm now facing Ms. Kestrel as she stands on the wagon bench. Her eyes are held open wide, and her hand covers her mouth as she tries to suppress her laughter. An ache runs down my leg as I step forward, tensing my body as it registers the pain.

"I'm going to butcher him. That meathead is as good as dead. In fact, he's on his own today. Can't get into the pen if nobody is here to open the gate," I growl through gritted teeth.

Jareth takes the reins from me, laughing at the look of determination on my face. "Now that we've gotten Tillard's shenanigans out of the way, let's try only to have gentle adventures today, hmm?"

As we head towards town, nervousness runs through me, leaving me nauseous. I know Ms. Kestrel has told me about everyone's reactions thus far, but the fear of negative responses brings with it a wave of self-doubt that threatens to wreck the hard work I've done when it comes to loving myself.

My nerves only increase as we step through Market District's gates. It's much busier today than I had expected it to be when we were talking last night, and much to my surprise, everyone seems to be lining up at...

Surely not. Am I seeing things? I rub my eyes, hoping to clear out whatever is in them that's making me hallucinate. The sight is still there when I lower my hands, and I reconcile that the number of people hovering at Number One Booth is really there, presumably waiting for our arrival.

"What is going on?" I ask Kaida, my voice low.

She shakes her head in disbelief, as though she's struggling to accept it, as well. "I don't know, Ellie. Are they really all at our booth? All of them?" She takes a sharp breath in before biting her lip.

When we step onto our side of the table, the crowd cheers, and one by one, we answer everyone's questions revolving around our farm. One person haggles a deal: the season's worth of vegetables, split into four deliveries, with payment up front for all at once. Another thanks me for my kindness, telling me they heard of our plans through the grapevine.

Before we reach the two-hour mark since opening, Jareth has made two trips to the wagon to restock, his gangly arms carrying as much as possible. Before my eyes, the produce vanishes instantly under a flood of purchases and requests.

By day's end, we've sold three times more produce than bakery goods, a first for us. Not only that, but we're also going home completely empty-handed for the first time, other than the baskets and crates we brought our wares in. I've been perpetually blown away today, the town increasingly excited by my plans for the season. I was even told that my idea is the best thing Smallburrow has seen in a generation, and not a single soul has objected.

Never in my wildest dreams did I think my spur-of-the-moment idea would cause so much goodness, especially in such a chaotic way, and for the first time in my life, I'm not dreading the thought of leading something so significant and life-changing.

It forces me to stop and take a moment to be thankful for the home I have found in Smallburrow. It's an achievement I don't think I would ever have been able to earn in Galbassi, even though I was a lifelong resident before moving here. It's only now that it occurs to me of the very real possibility my Grandpa Mapleground may have possessed a touch of clairvoyancy. In leaving me the farm, he must have known it was going to be precisely what I needed all along. My eyes burn from tears at this, though I quickly blink them away, silently thanking him for the lessons this journey has taught me.

Epilogue

Two days after our market sell-out, I wake up to find the ground covered by a thick, glistening blanket of snow. When I step onto the toasty floor, I'm immediately grateful Kaida and I had the foresight to keep the fireplace and woodstove lit, just in case. The heat from downstairs settles over the top floor, gently keeping me from turning into an ice block as I prepare for the day.

Quietly, I sneak down the stairs, hoping I don't wake Kaida or ruin my surprise. Once I tend the animals, I saddle up Mabel, and we head off into town.

Hopefully this won't take too long, since I've already done most of the prep, but I still want to be home when she wakes. The anticipation of seeing her reaction is killing me, and I've almost ruined everything more times than I can count.

I focus on the slushy sounds Mabel's hooves create as they trot through snow, visibly buzzing with excitement when I walk into Urzal's office, where both she and the mayor sit, waiting for me. After seeing Kaida stand in front of the building at the edge of Market District, I formulated a plan and roped both orcs into it. Which, it turns out, wouldn't have been difficult under any circumstances, not once Mayor Luddie learned of Kaida's desire to open a bakery in the currently vacant storefront. The cherry on top, though, is the hefty discount we're getting on the monthly payments due to how much Kaida and I have brought to Smallburrow, even in our short time of living here.

I take out the heavy coin purse from my pocket and hand it to them. "This is for the first four months. I don't want Kaida to worry about anything as she's getting everything together and running. There may be extra in there, I'm not sure. I tried to count it out as accurately as I could without making her suspicious."

Urzal laughs at my honesty. "It's a pleasure doing business with you. She is going to be thrilled."

Within minutes, I have the contract in hand, and the three of us are walking out the door. All it needs is Kaida's signature, and the deal will be complete. After shaking their hands, I smile at them. "I'll return this tomorrow afternoon, once she's looked everything over and has signed it," I promise as Urzal gives me an affectionate hug.

I must be delirious, because I practically skip across the lot with excitement. Suddenly, I come to a stop as I slam into a warm, breathing, brick wall. Mortification sweeps through me before I look up and see that, to my relief, the wall is none other than Jareth. I guess we can consider this payback from the Autumn Festival.

He steps back, startled by our collision. He relaxes when he realizes it's me and wipes the nonexistent sweat from his forehead. "Oh, it's you, Eilaen. You're up fairly early, huh?"

"I, uh, had an errand to run this morning. Needed to see Urzal and Mayor Luddie bright and early," I stammer, not wanting to risk ruining my surprise before I've even made it home.

He laughs. "I see that. By the way, when is Kaida's birthday? I know it's coming up, and I want to make sure she's on the town's birthday list."

"The middlest day of winter," I respond, giving him a tight smile. I want to explode. I want to tell him what I'm doing. I need to get home so I don't end up doing the very thing I've tried so hard not to do for days now. "Are you still coming to dinner tonight?"

He nods, giving me a quizzical look before telling me he'll see me later, and I practically run away from him so I can get home. Mabel carries me as quickly as she can, but I can't help counting the minutes that I'm losing. I'm running out of time to get there before Kaida wakes up, and it's all because I wasn't watching where I was going.

I smell the hazelnut chocolate rolls drifting outside before I make it into the yard. "Darn it, Mabel, we're just a little too late."

I quickly unsaddle the horse, giving her a good rub down before running into the house with the contract tucked in the inner pocket of my cloak. As I close the door, I yell Kaida's name, her response coming from the kitchen.

"Kai, sit on that stool. I have something exciting I want to give you," I command, slightly breathless.

"What's gotten into you this morning, Ellie? You're vibrating more than a honey bee in the spring," she replies, laughing.

I slip my hand under my cloak. "Close your eyes and hold out your hands." Pulling the rolled parchment out from its hiding place, I place it into her waiting palms. "Now, open."

Her head cocks to the side as she examines the paper she's holding. For the first time in her life, she has no expression to tell me what she thinks, and time ceases as she unrolls it to read.

I'm going to die if she doesn't say something, anything, in the next few minutes.

"Well, Kai. What do you think?"I ask timidly.

She looks at me, and her emotions flow from her eyes before anything else. "Ellie, this might be the nicest, most spectacular thing that anyone has ever done for me."

Pulling her into a hug, I breathe in relief. "Don't puddle yet because there's a little more. You won't have to worry about paying the rent for the first four months. It's already been taken care of. Happy early birthday, Kai. You've helped me with my dream. Now it's time to work on yours. Together."

She clutches me to her tighter, her sobs shaking us both. After wiping her nose and tears with her apron, she discards it and ties a new one around her as she tries to compose herself. For the rest of the day, we discuss her plans for the new bakery, Kaida throwing her hands around animatedly as we do.

Four months ago, I wasn't sure I wanted to come here to look, let alone live here. But after seeing how Kaida and I have both thrived, I cannot imagine doing it any other way.

Yes, I've been stretched thinner than ever, and yes, I battle that stupid pig almost daily. But it's moments like these, moments that make it all worth it.

It's in the moments where I find love in a family, where I learn new skills, and where I uncover the magic that's always been inside of me. This farm has already given me so much, and I know it has much more to give.

I now have a home, a family, and a sense of belonging. The possibilities for my future are now endless, and as I watch Kaida sketching her dream kitchen, I cannot wait to see where the road takes us next.

Eilaen's Diary

Entry from Eilaen's diary, dated the last day of autumn, year one as owner of Mapleground Farm.

I have learned many lessons already, some large and some small. But this one, dear diary, is the most important yet.

Family, I have come to learn, can come in all flavors. Sometimes you're born into it. Sometimes your family looks like you. But sometimes, your family finds you and picks you up out of your ashes, sweeps you off, and helps you back onto your feet. Sometimes, the best family that you will ever have is the one that finds you and accepts you just as you are, flaws and all.

Tillard's POV
(Bonus Epilogue)

Oink oink oink. Snort oink oink snort.
Squeal, oink, oiiiiiiink. Oink oink, oink, snort.
Snort snort, squeal, oink snort oink.
Sniff.
Oink, oink, oink.

Acknowledgements

To my husband and children, especially my Bee, thank you for your love and support. Having you guys to cheer me on has been the reason I keep going so much of the time, and I am so incredibly thankful for the seven of you.

To my editor, Lyss, thank you for standing by me from the beginning, even when I make you want to pull your hair out because I like to have too many ideas at once.

To my PA, Bianca, I am so incredibly thankful for your friendship and for you never failing to listen when I say "okay, so hear me out." I cannot wait to see us grow together.

To Amber at Bibliobean Publishing, thank you for taking on my little cozy fantasy tale. It means so, so much to me.

To my Chaos sisters--Audrey, Stephanie, and Chelsey--you guys have been in my corner since the conception of this series. Thank you for your love and support. I'd be lost without y'all.

To my Fated Mates street team, thank you for being my hype crew and for pushing me further every day. I am so thankful to have y'all in my corner.

And lastly, to my readers, thank you for picking up this book and choosing to spend time in Smallburrow. You will never know how incredible I think it is that you saw my book and said "I wanna read *this* one."

About the Author

T. M. Mayfield is a small-town author who loves all things fantasy. She is currently working to make her dream of being a fantasy author come true. When she isn't writing or editing, you can find her snuggling one of her cats, homeschooling her self-created army, or playing games with her true-life soulmate. She's also waiting for the day that Sonic: America's Drive-In realizes she can give them plenty of advertising and decides they want to sponsor her editing necessity drink habit.

You can also find her on Instagram with the handle @seetaylorwrite, Tiktok with the handle @seetaylorwrite, or on Facebook by searching T. M. Mayfield, Fantasy Author.

Also by T. M. Mayfield

The Stonemaw Chronicles

The River Queen
The Fae's Deceit
The Prophecy Unravels - Releasing late Spring 2026

The Halflings of Smallburrow:

Buried in Friendship
Dusted in Snowflakes
Rooted in Magic - Releasing April 2026
Soaked in Sunshine - Releasing August 2026

The Happily Ella After Duet:

Once Upon an Ella
Happily Ella After - Releasing Fall 2026

Standalones

Lady Azalea
Relics, Rivals, & Rage

www.ingramcontent.com/pod-product-compliance
Lightning Source LLC
Chambersburg PA
CBHW031052310726

48969CB00007B/2240